Kx

TOYS

JAMES PATTERSON is one of the best-known and biggest-selling writers of all time. He is the author of some of the most popular series of the past decade – the Alex Cross, Women's Murder Club and Detective Michael Bennett novels – and he has written many other number one bestsellers including romance novels and stand-alone thrillers. He lives in Florida with his wife and son.

James is passionate about encouraging children to read. Inspired by his own son who was a reluctant reader, he also writes a range of books specifically for young readers. James has formed a partnership with the National Literacy Trust, an independent, UK-based charity that changes lives through literacy. In 2010, he was voted Author of the Year at the Children's Choice Book Awards in New York.

Also by James Patterson

STAND-ALONE THRILLERS

Sail (*with Howard Roughan*)

Swimsuit (*with Maxine Paetro*)

Don't Blink (*with Howard Roughan*)

Postcard Killers (*with Liza Marklund*)

Now You See Her (*with Michael Ledwidge*)

Kill Me If You Can (*with Marshall Karp*)

Guilty Wives (*with David Ellis,
to be published July 2012*)

A list of more titles by James Patterson is printed at
the back of this book on pages 450–1

JAMES PATTERSON
& NEIL McMAHON
TOYS

arrow books

Published by Arrow Books in 2012

1 3 5 7 9 10 8 6 4 2

Copyright © James Patterson, 2011

James Patterson has asserted his right under the Copyright, Designs and Patents
Act, 1988 to be identified as the author of this work

First published in Great Britain in 2011 by Century

Arrow Books
Random House, 20 Vauxhall Bridge Road,
London SW1V 2SA

www.randomhouse.co.uk

Addresses for companies within The Random House Group Limited can be found at:
www.randomhouse.co.uk/offices.htm

The Random House Group Limited Reg. No. 954009

A CIP catalogue record for this book
is available from the British Library

Penguin Random House is committed to a sustainable future for
our business, our readers and our planet. This book is made from
Forest Stewardship Council® certified paper.

Typeset by SX Composing DTP, Rayleigh, Essex, SS6 7XF

Printed and bound in Great Britain by Clays Ltd, St Ives plc

Chapter 2

AS LIZBETH AND I entered the glittering ballroom, Westmont DeLong, the world's most popular and most celebrated comedian, was at center stage, entertaining with his droll patter of antihuman jokes. When he noticed that the audience was momentarily paying more attention to Lizbeth and me than to him, he raised his voice to win them back.

"Listen to this one, folks. Eyes on me, gents— ladies too! Right *here*, you and me.... The star is up on the stage.

"So an Elite's out for a night on the town. He has a few too many, and he wanders into a tavern in a borderline human zone," DeLong announced with his trademark sly grin.

"He buys a drink—then says to the people around him, 'I've got to tell you the best human joke I've heard in years.' The tough-looking woman bartender gets in his face. She says, 'Listen, buddy, I'm a martial arts expert, my boyfriend next to you is a professional no-gravity wrestler, and the bouncer is ex–Special Forces. All three of us are *humans* and—guess what?—there are *fifty* others like us in here. You really want to tell that joke?' 'No, forget it,' the Elite says. 'It would take me all night to explain it fifty-three times.'"

The crowd laughed loudly. Clearly, they were fans of Westmont DeLong—as was I—and a barrage of antihuman quips sprang up:

"One human asks another which is closer, the moon or Mexico," someone called out. "The second one points at the moon and says, 'Duh—you can't *see* Mexico from here.'"

"Scientists have started using humans instead of rats for laboratory experiments. They breed faster, and you don't get so attached to them."

DeLong chuckled and contributed, "Know what happens when humans don't pay their garbage bill? The company stops delivery."

"Come on, Hays, your turn," said a voice behind me. "Let's see that quick wit of yours in action. Dazzle us."

The tall, athletic, and handsome man who'd spoken was none other than Jax Moore, the head of the Agency of Change, where Lizbeth and I both worked. Moore was enjoying one of his trademark cigars—smokeless, odorless.

Everyone around us went quiet and watched expectantly. Since the challenge came from our boss, I couldn't duck it, could I? So I smoothed the lapels of my tux, smiled, and told the best human joke that I could remember.

"Well, there's an office full of human workers. One human woman notices that her boss, who's also a woman, is leaving early just about every day," I said. "So the worker decides she can get away with it too. That afternoon, she waits until the boss leaves, waits another ten minutes, and then sneaks out herself. But when she gets home, she hears an awful commotion coming from her bedroom. She peeks in—and there's her boss *in bed with her husband!*"

I paused, just a beat—pretty good timing, I was sure.

"She hurries back to work. 'Well, I'm not going to try *that* again,' she tells her coworkers. 'I almost got caught!'"

The room echoed with genuine laughter, and Westmont DeLong's face reddened. His double chin sagged as well. Lizbeth managed to look appropriately blasé, like she'd heard it all before, but she shot me a surreptitious wink that said, *Way to go, Hays.*

"Not bad, Hays," Moore said. "OK, if you can spare a minute or two away from the limelight, the president wants to see you both."

The president! Lizbeth didn't look blasé at that news. Neither of us had ever met President Jacklin before. This was a huge honor, of course.

"We don't usually give interviews without an appointment...but we'll make an exception in this case," I said.

"I'm sure the president will be flattered," Jax Moore said wryly. "And Hays—no more jokes. Not even human ones."

Chapter 3

"MY, MY. THE *PRESIDENT* wants to meet us," Lizbeth whispered in my ear as we followed Jax Moore farther into the mansion.

"Of course he does," I said with a grin.

Actually, Lizbeth and I *were* considered stars at that particular moment in time. We'd just returned from New Vegas, where we had saved countless lives while arresting a gang of moderately clever human bank robbers who had been terrorizing the West.

Anyway, Jax Moore whisked us through eight-foot-tall carved oak doors that led to the mansion's private living area. Well-concealed scanners examined every pore of our bodies as we walked to the entrance of the president's oval office, which was modeled after the famous original in the now-sunken city of Washington, DC.

I was immediately reminded that humans had created some good things in the past, such as this fine neoclassic style of architecture. But they'd also severely ravaged the planet, hadn't they? A couple decades ago the first generation of Elites had barely managed to save it from total destruction. Washington, DC, was one of many cities on the casualty list, along with most of the low-lying eastern seaboard, including New York City, Boston, and Philadelphia, all of which had been swallowed up long ago by the rising oceans.

When we stepped into the Oval Office, President Hughes Jacklin was standing in front of a full-length mirror, fumbling with his cravat. At his side was his faithful bodyguard and supposed lover, a behemoth named Devlin.

Seeing us, the president let the tie go and strode across the room to greet Lizbeth and me as if we were old friends. He was a hugely impressive man, classically educated, firm-jawed and broad-shouldered, and his thick dark hair was just beginning to gray at the temples.

"My dear, the sun is down and it's still as bright as day around you," he said to Lizbeth, kissing her perfect cheeks, one, then the other.

"Mr.—Mr. President," Lizbeth stammered ever so slightly, "I'm speechless…almost, anyway."

"What you are is incredibly charming," countered the president.

He turned to me and gave a firm handshake. "Hays Baker, this is a great pleasure. *You're* beautiful too. Look, I'm late for my own party— we'll have time to get better acquainted later. But I want you to know I've followed your careers at the Agency closely. And I'm a big fan. That operation in Vegas was pure genius. Efficient and effective. Just what I like."

"We're proud to help, Mr. President," Lizbeth said, actually blushing a little now.

"Then would you help me out with *this* thing?" He flapped the loose ends of his cravat with good-humored exasperation. "I never could get the hang of it. Or the significance of ties, damn them."

"I could do that," said Devlin, but the president waved the bodybuilding bodyguard away.

"Lizbeth?" he said, exposing his throat to her. "Let's see how you would *garrote* a world leader."

Chapter 4

"IT WOULD BE my pleasure, sir!"

Lizßeth laughed like an impressionable school-girl and took over. As her nimble fingers arranged the president's tie into an expert knot, he gave us a conspiratorial nod. Off to the side, Devlin was grimacing and fidgeting, and I hoped we hadn't made an enemy of the giant bodyguard.

"I will tell you this much about my future plans," the president said. "My best people have developed a program to—let's just say, *complete* the work of making our world a safer, cleaner place with respect to the human strain. We'll be launching it soon. In *days,* actually."

Lizbeth and I had heard rumors that a sweeping human-containment initiative had been taking shape. It was hard not to be relieved. The foolhardy and dangerous humans had only themselves to blame. They had blown their chance to make the world a better place. It was undeniable that they had accomplished quite the opposite.

"I'm counting on you both for important help with the launch of the human cleanup. Meantime, you're the best we have at holding the gross and undesirable elements in check. Please keep up the good work. Bigger, better things are coming for you two. For all Elites, actually." He checked himself in the mirror. "Come to think of it—humans are responsible for *ties!*"

President Jacklin smiled, then he said goodbye with effusive warmth—he was obviously an expert at it, perhaps aided by the prototype Cyrano 3000 implant he was rumored to have. I'd only read about the device, but what I knew was that it was surgically attached to a person's inner ear and could offer guidance through any social interaction. The amazing appliance had wireless access to a database of pretested social cues, pertinent information about whatever person you were talking to, and other useful facts, names, quotes, and quips that might fit a given situation. The irony: a human had also invented it.

Jax Moore took my elbow, then Lizbeth's, and walked us back to the oak doors. He lit up another of his cigars and puffed contentedly.

"Not a word about this. There can be no security leaks. Check with me first thing tomorrow," he said. "I have classified information we need to discuss. The president specifically asked for you two on the 'human problem.' You're both...*beautiful*," Moore closed, giving us an icy grin that could have frozen vegetables. I doubted he'd undergone a Cyrano 3000 implant, or even heard of it.

After the doors closed, Lizbeth took my arm and said, "One of the best nights of our lives, don't you think?" She'd handled the president with perfect poise—and charm—but she was also clearly starstruck after meeting the great man in person. To be honest, so was I. I just didn't let on.

"Definitely in the top hundred or so," I teased her.

"*Really*," she said archly. "You'll have to remind me of the others. Such as?"

"How about the night when we met? Michigan Avenue, New Chicago."

She laughed. "Hmmm. Well, that *might* be in the top hundred."

"I guess I asked for that," I said as we exchanged a kiss that I'm sure caused a whistle or two in the president's security-camera control room.

Chapter 5

WHAT CAUGHT MY attention next was the incredible number of high-ticket toys at the party.

Sometimes it seemed like toys were all the world cared about in the second half of the twenty-first century. Humans and Elites had both fallen under their spell and become addicted to the endless pleasures and nonstop excitement they could provide. And the toys were only getting better, or worse, depending on your point of view.

Even in the presidential mansion—where you might think the serious business of the country would be getting done 24-7—toys were playing a big part in the celebration. Wide-eyed, deep-pocketed guests were crowded around a display where employees from Toyz Corporation were giving demos of some of the choicer items in the forthcoming, but thus far unreleased, catalog.

As Lizbeth and I reentered the ballroom, we were surrounded by a menagerie of cloned, genetically tamed animals—birds of paradise, Galápagos tortoises, enormous butterflies, pygmy hippos—and then we almost got knocked over by a beautiful woman in a gold gown and matching high heels, who was laughing while riding on a thick-maned lion.

"Oops, sorry," she said breathlessly as she raced by. Then she called over her shoulder to Lizbeth, "You've *got* to try this, Liz. You've never felt such *muscles*."

"Now that's certainly not true," Lizbeth whispered as her hand delicately grazed my upper leg. "My beauty."

Other women were draping defanged cobras and wondrously patterned tropical vipers around their necks like mink stoles, and one demented man showed off by thrusting his head into the jaws of a docile baby *Tyrannosaurus rex*. I almost wished the toy would take a bite.

While Lizbeth admired the fauna—Elite and otherwise—I stepped up to a bank of SimStims, the hugely popular and addictive simulators that offered a variety of different experiences, all so intensely real that it was illegal to sell SimStim machines to anyone with a heart condition. You could choose from any number of simulations — have passionate sex with a movie or government star, for example, rock out onstage surrounded by a vast audience of screaming fans, or fight for your life in the heat of combat.

I slipped on a mood helmet at one of the simulators and scanned the on-screen menu. The range of choices was staggering: Moorish Harem, Eye of a Hurricane Experience, Pagan Barbarities, Tennis vs. the Pro, Pig Out: No Calories, Death Experience: A Final 60 Seconds, Visit Your Former Lives.

Movie buff that I am, I picked the general heading of Great Moments in Cinema.

I barely glimpsed the words "This Program Has Been Edited for Your Enhanced Pleasure," and then I was *there*. Bogie in *Casablanca*.

I gazed into the liquid blue eyes of Ingrid Bergman sitting across from me — then I raised my whiskey glass to touch hers.

"Here's looking at you, kid," I said, losing myself in her answering smile.

Then the door of the noisy café burst open and a toadlike little man ran in, looking around in panic. The great human character actor Peter Lorre had arrived.

"Rick, you have to help me," he gasped in a heavy accent, thrusting a sheaf of papers at me. "Hide these!"

I strode to the piano as he rushed out the back door, and I had just managed to shove the papers under the lid when gunshots sounded in the street outside. Suddenly, jackbooted soldiers stormed in—

My heart raced, and I felt myself instinctively backing away toward the bar. There was a Luger right there under the counter.

This was amazing. I was living Bogie's part in the film masterpiece. And then—surprise of surprises...

Chapter 6

I FOUND MYSELF staring at the menu screen, a little miffed at the next message. "Presented by Toyz Corporation," it blinked in stark black and white. "We hope you'll come back soon."

"Great," I sighed. "Well, it did say great *moments* in cinema, didn't it?"

Lizbeth was watching me with folded arms and raised eyebrows as I removed the mood helmet.

"Have a good time?" she asked and started to grin mischievously.

"A little short-lived," I said, wondering if any of the other programs were full-length—maybe next time I'd get into something like a Viking raid, or maybe visit that Moorish harem.

Actually, I was quite a student of human history. I never would have turned the government back over to them, but if one thing's true about the *Homo sapiens*, it's that they almost *never* let you down in the drama department. I mean the scandals, the three World Wars, the artistic movements, games, literature, films…and the music! I adored Mozart, but also Bob Dylan and Edith Piaf.

I took Lizbeth's hand and we strolled back toward the center of the great hall.

"Let's take a look at those dolls. I want to see if they're suitable for April and Chloe," she said. "They're absolutely *begging* for them, Hays."

"They have more than enough toys already," I said, but quickly relented. "Oh all right, Jinx. I can't say no to them."

Lizbeth pointed at a demonstration of the season's hottest new items—Jessica and Jacob dolls, beautiful miniature androids that looked and acted perfectly lifelike. Kids everywhere—including our own two daughters—were causing parents to line up around the block to purchase them at Toyz stores all over the country.

The clever display was set up in a series of

tableaux—separate scenes of home, office, store, and restaurant—with dozens of the lifelike dolls chatting, working, and eating just like real people, though only sixteen inches tall.

To be perfectly honest, while I couldn't quite take my eyes off them, I found the dolls more than a little creepy.

But the crowd was riveted, especially a growing knot in front of a sign that read THESE MODELS SPECIAL ORDER ONLY.

When Lizbeth and I strolled over there, we immediately saw why.

"Oh my," she said. "Oh dear, Hays. That's just gross."

Underneath the sign was a doll-sized bed where a Jake and Jessie in the buff were thrashing around in primal delight. I mean, those two were really going at it.

"I guess we can scratch the special orders off our list," Lizbeth said.

"They really *can* do everything. Energetic little devil, isn't he?"

Lizbeth rolled her eyes. "There's more to it than slamming in and out like a piston. Don't you think, Hays? I'll bet you anything these dolls were programmed by a man—and probably one between the ages of sixteen and thirty-five. They should let a woman redo the code if they really want them to sell."

"Thinking about volunteering?" I said. Biocircuitry was Lizbeth's specialty—she was one of the foremost experts at the Agency of Change. "And what would you do differently, dear heart? Have all the Jacobs look like me?"

Her lips brushed my ear. "That's not such a terrible idea, Hays. Say, I'm thinking this party has served its official purpose for us," she murmured. "What do you say we go home? Maybe play some games of our own?"

"Umm, coming through," I said, taking her hand and leading her off the crowded floor. The best night of our professional lives was about to get even better, and on a much more intimate level.

Jinxie and I were going home.
Yippee!

Chapter 7

THIS WAS WHERE the slope began to get slippery, dangerously slippery indeed.

Outside the presidential mansion, more iJeeves butlers were escorting rich and famous guests to a long line of waiting limos. Lizbeth and I were soon settled back in our Agency-loaned driverless vehicle to enjoy the air ride through the beautiful Elite zone of New Lake City.

Glittering hundred-story buildings stretched out before us for miles, with impossibly fast-moving flying cars, trucks, and buses streaking between them. As Jinxie had said earlier, *We really do run the world*. In truth, we Elites had saved the planet, so why not?

Off toward the outskirts of the high-rises,

you could see the dark gaps of the human slums. Sad stuff, even if you despised the humans. But maybe the president's plan would fix that once and for all. The humans had proved they couldn't be trusted under any circumstances.

Lizbeth and I snuggled together like giddy teenagers inside the limo, whetting our appetites for later on. She kept making jokes about how "beautiful" I was.

"I want you to try the new Rapture pill, Hays. Two-minute orgasms."

"Contact your physician if orgasm lasts an hour or longer," I said as I leaned in for a kiss.

Then—out of nowhere—it felt like a giant boulder had crashed into the roof of the Daimler. The impact buckled the incredibly strong titanium roof, rocking us from side to side, then bringing the car to a graceless, airbag-assisted landing on the street below.

"Hays?" Lizbeth said in alarm. "Are we being attacked? We are, aren't we? *How dare they?*"

At first I could see nothing outside the smashed-open windows. But I definitely heard yelling and pounding feet. Five, six, seven people coming toward us—fast.

Even as I ordered the limo to disengage our safety restraints, I could smell their foul body odor. *Humans*. Damn them. They must have crashed another vehicle on top of ours and forced us down, and they were now moving in for the kill. Robbery, of course, possibly rape—for both of us.

Like all Elites, I thoroughly distrusted humans. They were terminally lazy and stupid, and their flesh reeked of the greasy food they gobbled. The popular Elite term for them was *skunks*, although they were a bit more like hyenas, or wild dogs, in terms of the lives they led. Violence, deceit, and opportunism ruled their petty days and nights, just as it had through most of history. Hell, they had even written books about it, from Horace and Homer to Thomas Friedman and Stieg Larsson.

As Agents of Change, Lizbeth and I were dedicated to bringing fairness and justice to their barbaric ways and making them pay for their crimes. An act this outrageous—entering a restricted-access area and actually attacking Elites—made these vandals candidates for the harshest penalty there was: *slow death*.

I could see now that they were an ugly bunch,

even for humans: grim-faced and menacing, armed with knives and scalpel-sharp box cutters, plus a few old-fashioned handguns.

My threat-assessment sensors instantly ranked their strength from lowest to highest. Three of them, I noted immediately, had biotech upgrades: enhanced musculature, joints, and reflexes. It wasn't commonplace, but it was possible—through bioengineering—to augment a human to nearly Elite levels of power and conditioning.

"Shall we?" I asked Lizbeth. Besides being a doctor of engineering and possessing a genius-level IQ, my beautiful wife was a deadly hand-to-hand fighter. Besides being a doctor of history, I was also.

"I wish I'd worn sensible shoes," Lizbeth said as she glanced at her party pumps and grimaced.

Chapter 8

I WRENCHED OPEN the limo door on my side, using it as a shield to clear a path as I leaped out. Lizbeth followed close behind, one of her shapely legs flashing from under her evening gown as she planted a spiked heel in a punk's ear. He staggered away, howling in great pain.

"Drop your weapons!" I yelled in warning.

They didn't, of course. What a surprise.

So I began with the weakest-ranked assailant in my reach, slipping aside as he charged at me swinging a nasty-looking box cutter. I snapped the skunk's wrist and tossed him across the street against a lamppost. He hit with a doughy crack—as an empty beer bottle wrapped in clay would—and slid down to the pavement.

I briefly wondered if he'd had a chance to hear the thud when his skull shattered.

The next piece of human scum charged, screeching like a savage beast. I feinted a lunge, then somersaulted over him, dislocating both his shoulders in midflight.

"Three of them are fully augmented," I cautioned Lizbeth.

"Got it, Hays. Thanks, darling. I'll take it easy on them."

My next foe was a fast learner, and clearly had undergone impressive augmentations. Instead of fighting, he ran—or pretended to. It took me all of three 10-foot strides to catch him.

As my hand lashed out to crush the elbow of his knife arm, he whipped around at me like a snake—a preternaturally fast snake—holding a second knife in his other hand. It sliced past my throat so fast I could hear the whir of the blade through the air.

"Close, guy. I'm impressed." I gave him his due.

Then I followed the arc of his knife with my own slashing left hand, slapping the weapon out of his grasp as my right hand crushed his other elbow from behind. Next, I jammed his head between two vertical bars in one of the neighborhood's iron fences and bent them around his neck to form a snug, but not quite strangling, collar.

"Not to worry," I said. "The police will be here to rescue you soon."

I absolutely needed to keep a couple of these skunks alive for interrogation. Had to keep that in mind.

I glanced over at Lizbeth to make sure she was doing OK. My lovely bride was just dispatching her next assignment with a graceful rib-cage-collapsing ballet kick. In her spare time, she's a dancer, a private dancer for the kids and me.

"Way to go, Dr. Baker!" I called to her.

"You too, Dr. Baker!"

I turned my attention to the last of the group, the one who had registered on my sensors as far and away the most dangerous. The criminal was still in the driver's seat of the car they'd rammed into ours—he only watched while the others fought. *Coward, or mastermind?* I wondered. *If there is such a thing as a human mastermind.*

Only it wasn't a he, I suddenly realized. The

creep's shaggy blond hair was cut short, but the body and facial structure was definitely female.

She was staring at me through the open car window, and the emotion she projected, the undisguised hatred in her eyes, made my scalp bristle. Then she completely shocked me—she knew my name.

"You think you're a hero, Hays Baker, but you have no idea what you're doing," she said softly. "*You're* the criminal here."

Then she pulled back on the car's wheel and it accelerated straight skyward. My muscles tensed to leap and catch hold of the rear bumper. I could have done it. But I stayed rooted to the ground. I had no idea why.

Lizbeth was watching me, suddenly looking concerned. "Hays, are you hurt?" she called. "*Hays?*"

"No, I'm...I'm fine."

She looked puzzled. "Why didn't you go after the driver?"

"I...I thought it was too risky," I said, though that wasn't it at all. "If the car had taken off and we'd crashed...we're in a residential neighborhood. Don't worry, we'll catch her."

"*Her? It was a woman?*" Lizbeth asked in amazement. "I thought all human females were pregnant and working behind a stove."

"Good one, Jinxie," I said and gave her a hug. She could tell a human joke with the best of them.

Chapter 9

THE LOCAL POLICE arrived in the next sixty seconds and very quickly and professionally cordoned off the automobile crash and crime scene. The Agency had already been in touch to verify our vitals and to dispatch another car to take Lizbeth and me home.

We arrived at our apartment, a beautiful tenth-story floor-through in one of the most desirable lakefront locations in the city.

When we stepped through our front door, the first thing we heard was the jangly, atonal pulse of robo-rap music coming from our house android, Metallico, who was prancing around the living room and singing along with the tunes.

Metallico hastily turned off the sound and

stared at us in shock. "What in the world happened to you two?" he asked. "Lizbeth, your beautiful hair is a mess!"

"Never mind about that," she snapped. "What happened to *this* place? It looks like all the closets exploded."

"Well, excuse *me*. I suppose I'm too lazy to shop, cook, play nanny, *and* clean, all at the same time. If you must know, I just finished giving the girls their bath and was starting to tidy up. I wasn't expecting you home so early." The robot's supple, bronze-tinted silicone skin glowed a little brighter, indicating his annoyance.

"We had a slight change of plans," I said calmly. I always tried to smooth over these little sniping matches between the two of them.

The apartment didn't seem all that bad to me; Lizbeth had a tendency toward tidiness that could go over the edge. There were games and clothes strewn on the coffee table, but Metallico was right: with our two little-girl cyclones racing around at full speed, even he—a machine designed to clean—sometimes got maxed out before day's end.

His skin had returned to a normal hue,

although he still managed to convey that his "feelings" had been hurt.

"All right, let's kiss and make up," he said. "I'll get you both a drink—you look like you could use it. Your clothes—*Lord*."

He gave us quick hugs and pecks on the cheek, then bustled off to the kitchen, crooning again, shaking his booty, and making us both smile, though Lizbeth did mutter "hopeless heap of metal" under her breath.

Besides being incredibly helpful, Metallico could be a lot of fun. He was the size and shape of a normal adult but built for work and, thus, without the refined exterior of the high-end entertainment androids. But he could move with such speed and grace that he made the simplest household task look like an Olympic event. He was also a perfect playmate and teacher for the girls, a vast encyclopedia of knowledge— robots like him were of course interfaced to the Cybernet, with all the information of our entire civilization at their instant command—a witty conversationalist, a master of adult games (such as four-dimensional chess), a gourmet chef, and a thousand other useful things. Also, like the rest of our family, he despised and distrusted all humans.

As he came back with our regular no-carb drinks — a glass of sauvignon blanc for Lizbeth, vodka with a twist for me — Chloe and April came charging into the room and threw themselves into our arms. *Ah, my sweet baby girls.*

"Did you bring us Jessica and Jacob dolls?" they asked their mom. Chloe, who'd just turned four, pronounced dolls *dows*. She was an elfin beauty with her mother's violet and ivory coloring, while April, six, was tawny-skinned with thick blond hair like mine.

"I'm not feeling very good about those dolls, sweeties," Lizbeth confessed.

"Neither am I," I added in support. "Sorry, ladies."

"Noooo," the girls wailed in a chorus of grief.

"We'll talk about it tomorrow, OK? It's bedtime — go get settled, and Daddy will come tell you a story. Won't you, Hays?"

"Of course I will. That's why they call me Daddy, isn't it?"

Chapter 10

ALTHOUGH DISAPPOINTED, the girls were mostly obedient at this age, and they scampered away to their room. "C'mon, Daddy!" they called to me. "You have to tell us a story now. *Two* stories. Because you're denying us our dolls."

I followed close behind and turned my thoughts to choosing a favorite bedtime story for my babies. I scrolled through the library menu on Chloe's wall . . . maybe *Don't Let the Pigeon Land the Car,* or *Mr. Popper's Penguins.*

The thing about the girls and me back then, we had sort of a secret life. On the weekends, we loved to go off to the city's very large library to read together. We listened to Mozart on earphones on the way there, then settled in to read

Charles Dickens aloud. The point—if there has to be a point to everything—is that you can hate humans, but nobody should hate Mozart or Charles Dickens or J. K. Rowling.

As I was reminiscing about our little secret times together, my earring phone chirped— three quick beeps signaled an Agency emergency of some sort. "Damn!" I muttered. "This can't be happening."

"Daddy!" April said with a frown. "You just said a forbidden word." I wasn't supposed to curse.

The caller turned out to be Owen McGill, my partner at the Agency of Change and a longtime friend, probably my best friend—other than Lizbeth, that is.

"Grab your boots, Hays," McGill said. "There's been an ugly incident at the Toyz store in Baronville"—a tony Elite suburb at the northern edge of New Lake City, about twenty miles away. "They want you here right now. It's homicides, *plural*."

"Me? Now? I already had my ugly incident for the night. Lizbeth and I were attacked—*by skunks*. Besides, I'm supposed to be off."

"Sorry, buddy. Jax Moore specifically requested you. 'I want Hays Baker on this!' That's what he said."

I exhaled. "All right, all right. I'm on my way."

So much for reading bedtime stories, a romantic interlude with my wife, or even getting to taste my vodka with a twist of lemon. What a letdown, and what a shit night this was turning out to be.

I hadn't even had time to take off my tux jacket before I was heading off to face, well, whatever was so important that Jax Moore had requested me at the crime scene.

Homicides — plural.

Chapter 11

OUR APARTMENT BUILDING'S superfast express elevator whisked me up to the rooftop garage, and I jumped into my own car—a teardrop-shaped sports-pod just big enough to comfortably fit me and a passenger. Although the touch of a button would extend it rearward, enabling it to carry as many as four others.

As the hatch slid shut, the instrument panel lights blinked a message: "Ready when you are, Dr. Baker."

"Toyz store, Baronville, max speed," I said.

Usually, I operated the vehicle myself, but right now I needed a break, even—as it would have to be in this case—a very short one.

"Roger that, Dr. Baker," replied the interactive pilot's crisp voice.

Suddenly, the sports-pod shot straight upward, then forward, pressing me firmly back into the custom seats. These superlight pods were among the fastest models available, capable of doing zero to sixty in two seconds flat, maneuvering in the air like a hummingbird, and cruising comfortably at three hundred miles per hour, even on a surface road.

"Airspace clearance is set. Estimated flight time: four minutes and twenty-three seconds," said a different voice, female and as familiar as an old friend. "Would you care for a drink? Entertainment of any kind? Sensory stimulation?"

This was Elle, the artificially intelligent attendant. I hadn't named the pilot—our relationship was more businesslike—but Elle deserved a name.

"How about some Bach?" I said. "Please, Elle. That would be terrific. Just what I need."

"If I might make a suggestion, the Brandenburg Number Six, Allegro, would just about fit our flight parameters."

"Perfect."

"Perhaps with a multisense track?" she said.

"Something light, yes."

Elle didn't have a full body, just a pair of slender robotic arms, but they functioned with a precise efficiency that could be spellbinding. She slipped the car's mood helmet onto my head, and I relaxed with the classical music—another of the very good things that humans had given the world. How bizarre was that?

Actually, to be fair, humans were still making a few worthwhile contributions to the world. We Elites weren't numerous enough to fill every role in our society, so we had to concentrate on managing the vital ones—government, medical, military, law enforcement, telecommunications, media. Consequently, well-trained and strictly supervised humans were still manning the orchestras, bands, and studio sessions that we required. Humans also had many necessary subservient roles, especially those involving cleaning and waste collection.

But I believed it was Elite technology that really took classical music to the next level— when the Brandenburg began, I wasn't just listening, I was *experiencing* with all my senses . . .

...drifting along a pure, clear river, with the scent of lilacs in spring wafting through the air.

Trees along the banks thrust their strong trunks up from the earth, while their branches reach like slender, red-tipped fingers to caress the sky.

Rich, ripe fruit of all varieties hang within easy reach, and alluring nymphlike shapes frolic in the water around me, waving at me to come join them in their play...

The exquisite concerto ended with its last, very memorable drawn-out chord.

"We're here, Dr. Baker," Elle said in the quietest whisper. "Toyz store, Baronville."

Damn. I could have used a little more Bach.

Chapter 12

OWEN MᴄGILL CERTAINLY hadn't exaggerated —the crime scene was ugly all right. Eleven dead! The first thing I saw was a butchered male body in what looked to be a very expensive navy blue pin-striped suit. The poor fellow's torso was twisted horribly and partly submerged in a veritable lake of his own blood.

I'd seen plenty of gore before, but this was possibly the worst yet. The most nightmarish aspect of the scene was that the victim's blood had splattered all over some miniature toy horses that had been let out of a stable-themed play set.

The cat-sized horses were covered head to hoof in blood and were walking around, leaving tiny, crescent-shaped red prints on the synthetic marble floor, apparently looking for some miniature oats or hay.

Creepy didn't begin to describe it.

But the full measure of the massacre, the carnage, was much worse than that initial impression.

A second corpse, this one female and partially dressed in an expensive gold lamé pantsuit, was lying nearby. Close to that were two more female victims. Their trademark pink and blue Toyz shopping bags were scattered everywhere around the courtyard.

They had been cut in a way that sickened me — torsos savagely ripped open, organs removed, the heads completely gone. *Missing*, in fact.

As I stared at the gore, and shooed away one of the little horses from the male's body, McGill came striding over. As always, I was glad to see him. My friend is rock solid, dependable, and a good ally when things get rough. He's built like a gorilla, six foot six, and close to three hundred pounds.

"Where are the killers?" I said, assuming the humans responsible had been arrested by now. The city police would have been on the case immediately.

"So far, no sign of them, Hays. You believe it? They got away with this."

"That's not possible."

"I hear you. Gets even stranger though. Listen to this. Every single one of the security cameras in the place *just happened* to malfunction at the same time."

"What?"

"It gets even better. There must have been close to a hundred customers in the store— nobody remembers a goddamn thing. Not even the security guards."

That was impossible. Elites have crystal clear memories and would never lie to authorities. They aren't capable of it.

"Go ahead, ask 'em," Owen McGill challenged me. He gestured at the civilians gathered beyond the cordon. "Maybe it will start coming back to them—once you turn on the old Hays Baker charm."

As with most of the company's consumer outlets, especially ones in respectable Elite communities, this Toyz superstore was open twenty-four hours, and it was crowded with customers.

"Who can tell me what happened?" I stepped forward and called to the blank-faced, clearly confused crowd. "Somebody must have seen these terrible murders. I need witnesses. Please. *Anybody?* Speak up now."

A pretty, young Elite woman, wearing skintight jeans and a bodice that barely covered her nipples, shrugged helplessly. "I was standing right there, looking at the iSpielberg imagers," she said, pointing at a display of equipment that allowed you to star in your own movie.

Her shaking finger moved toward the homicide scene.

"Those two—I don't think they were a couple…they acted more like they worked together…Anyhow, they were walking past me, talking to each other. It was all perfectly… ordinary. Then—they were lying on the floor. Just like they are now. Cut open! It's the weirdest thing, but it was like there was *nothing* in between."

Others in the crowd nodded their heads in complete agreement.

"Hey, why don't you tell *us* what's going on?" a man in front called out to me. "The police are supposed to protect us, aren't you? How could you let something like this happen? In a Toyz store of all places?"

It was a fair question, but I didn't have a clue what to say. How could I? Basically, *these murders just couldn't have happened.*

Chapter 13

"COME ON, THERE are more bodies up front," McGill said in a quiet voice, respectful of the occasion or, perhaps, the deeply disturbing mystery of it. It was rare for Elites to be crime victims—now here were eleven of them dead, and Lizbeth and I were still recovering from an armed attack. What the hell was going on?

I followed Owen through the distraction-crammed store, trying to keep my focus on the grisly task at hand and my head clear of the Toyz siren song.

But what a collection of playthings. Sex and adventure simulators, domestic servants that could do everything but think your thoughts, genetically tamed wild animals that never needed feeding, personal submarines, personal airpods, role-playing worlds, antigravity chambers, celebrity "clone" androids you could bring home and interact with as you pleased... *Toys, toys, toys for all good little girls and boys.* That line—from the Toyz store's famous jingle—you couldn't get it out of your head without using a ThoughtCleanser, another Toyz store favorite.

"One thing's for sure—it had to be skunks," McGill said grimly, hatred for the despicable human killers burning like hot coals in his eyes.

I nodded. No Elite would commit a vicious crime like this. Almost by definition, it's what separates us from those murdering animals. Genetically speaking, of course, Elites are more than 99 percent human. It's not something we tend to dwell on, but we're rational—and it is what it is.

Quite simply, our kind was geneered from human stock. In our case, it was deliberate science rather than blind natural selection—but it's essentially similar to how "modern" humans themselves are said to have evolved from *Homo erectus* or *Australopithecus* or other primitive forms.

But even more significant than our DNA blueprint—genes, after all, are simply sets of biological instructions—is the final product. Unlike humans—or any organism that's ever walked under the sun for that matter—we aren't just flesh and blood. We contain circuitry and nanomachinery. Although it isn't visible from the outside, we are, in fact, part machine.

One other difference between *us* and *them* is that rather than being born from a woman's uterus, we grow in artificial wombs. This means Elite women don't have to endure the old-world pain, inconvenience, and health risks of pregnancy.

Artificial wombs also permit us to gestate for longer—we spend a full two years developing before birth, as opposed to the typical nine months of human pregnancy. Among other things, this makes it possible for doctors to integrate the biocircuitry and other augmentations that enable us to rise above humankind's dangerous shortcomings: greed, immorality, self-destructiveness, rage. I could go on and on, of course. Even the best human artists understood humanity's frailties and failings. Just read Shakespeare, Dostoyevsky, Swift, Rand, Solzhenitsyn—even pop culture writers like Stephen King and Philip K. Dick got it right.

The brutally dismembered bodies at the Toyz store reminded me once again these human flaws should never be underestimated. Too often the outcome was tragic.

Looking around the scene, I noticed something interesting. The organs taken from the bodies were all those linked to uniquely Elite biotechnical augmentations—especially our circuitry-enhanced brains. It suggested something even more disturbing: the massacre at the store wasn't random, or motivated by robbery—this wasn't an explosion of shortsighted rebellion and rage that occasionally flares in the human ranks.

Instead, this had all the elements of a complex and premeditated murder plot.

I shook my head and walked the route between the two crime scenes, cataloging traces that the cold-blooded attackers had left.

They'd come in at the rear—the blood of the first corpses I'd seen was more congealed than the others—and they'd moved fast to execute their daring plan. Footprints in the blood—sizes ten and a half, twelve, and two size elevens, all popular-brand athletic shoes—told me that there'd been four of them. Large males. Animalistic. Acting without any regard for right or wrong.

A forensic team was on its way, but I already knew my assignment: I had to go bag myself four murdering skunks before they could kill again.

The Toyz premier items on display tonight were, of course, Jessica and Jacob dolls. Dozens of them had been placed in the store's huge front window, undoubtedly to lure in traffic. *Scary* didn't start to cover that tableau.

The dolls had wandered away from their display stations and were now standing behind the glass barrier.

They were staring at the mutilated Elite corpses, pointing at them, talking among themselves like so many looky-loos at a terrible, terrible traffic accident.

To the Jessicas and Jacobs, the crime scene seemed to be the featured amusement for tonight. Talk about disturbing—*dolls being entertained by real-life tragedy.*

Lizbeth was right—there was no way our

Chloe and April were going to get any of these little bastards for the holidays. Not while I was Dad.

Chapter 14

"DR. BAKER, *SIR*. Our street surveillance cameras have picked up four skunks on motorcycles fleeing the area," a city cop called out, hurrying toward me. "They're heading north along the lakefront. We have emergency units—"

I was already running for my car. I wanted in on this capture in the worst way. I had never investigated a crime as daring and unspeakable as this one.

This time I took over the driving controls. As I sped out onto the streets, I barked a command at the dashboard computer: "Four motorcycles, north lakefront. Rapid pursuit until intersect."

That order activated a link to the city's network of surveillance cameras.

Instantly, a grid appeared on-screen, showing a cluster of four shapes hunched over their bikes.

The readout gave their speed as 187 miles per hour and their location as 7.347 miles away. Other shapes on-screen showed me that airborne police pods were already chasing them and ground vehicles were forming roadblocks ahead.

The fact that they'd gotten as far as they had was astonishing and made me feel anything but secure about a peaceful arrest.

McGill's avatar suddenly appeared on my display. I blinked my eye at the communications icon, signaling the computer to pick up his call.

"Hays, we've ID'd the vics at the store," he reported to me now. "They were all Toyz Corp execs."

"What?"

"Yeah, and we're not talking district managers either. They were members of the Toyz board. Moore's crazed about it. So, you know, no pressure or anything. Just catch—and kill—the bastards. No mercy."

"I'm closing in on the vermin right now," I said, then clicked off McGill's feed with a blink.

No mercy indeed.

Chapter 15

I COULD DEFINITELY see the humans motoring at full speed up ahead. As if on cue, the cluster of bikes suddenly split apart, peeling off in different directions like campfire sparks scattered by high winds.

They dove down back alleys and even onto narrow walkways, where the maneuverable bikes could evade the roadblocks and stay sheltered from police aircraft. *Smart bastards.*

"Your muscle tension is extremely high, sir," observed Elle. "Would you like me to engage ultrasonic massage?"

"Not now, Elle — I'm skunkhunting."

"Of course, sir," she replied, and her status light turned from bright yellow to dim green. "Good luck with that."

I was getting close to the outskirts of the city and the chaotic human settlements where my targets would have a decent chance at disappearing among their kind of filth and vermin. What a terrible outcome that would be for the Agency — and for my own record.

I rammed the joystick forward and the pod went airborne, streaking up at a thirty-degree trajectory to an altitude of approximately one hundred feet. Then it leveled out.

Within seconds I was closing in on the nearest rider. I was doing more than twice his speed, actually. God, I wanted at him.

The punk killer was still on a fairly wide street, but he never had a chance to swerve away. I didn't give him one. I swooped down between the buildings and came in over him like an eagle snaring a gopher.

The car's belly grazed his back — just hard enough to flip him.

As I shot on by, the dashboard screen showed him skidding along the pavement, then bouncing wildly off several building fronts. *Good riddance to bad rubbish.*

At close to two hundred miles per hour, there

probably wouldn't be much left of that one.

The next closest rider was .74 miles away. The on-screen grid showed a path where I could stay hidden between buildings until I intercepted him.

I dropped the sports-pod back down onto the street and peeled out on a stretch of smooth concrete pavement.

Seconds later, I whipped around a tight corner in front of him—then skidded broadside to cut him off.

But he was good with a bike. I'll give him that much credit. He braked and laid the motorcycle down on its side, crouching on top and riding it like a sled.

At the last second, the rider leaped clear and tumbled away with the skill of a gymnast. The bike was still hurtling toward me, bouncing and throwing off sparks.

It slammed into my car hard enough to completely demolish the passenger side and send me violently off course.

Bright red warning lights flashed on the dashboard, and the shrill beep of an alarm sounded.

"We're under attack, sir!" the interactive pilot announced.

Sometimes artificial intelligence doesn't quite live up to its name.

Chapter 16

"*NO IMMEDIATE DANGER to personnel on board,*" chirped the pilot computer as the pod righted itself and avoided what would have been a most unpleasant, and possibly deadly, impact with the front of a tinny-looking warehouse. "*Damage to vehicle will not impair operation.*"

"No problem then," I muttered.

I swung the pod around in a tight arc and zeroed in on the running human. With a touch, I sent off a heat-seeking tracer round from my front gun port.

The skunk vanished in an explosion of red vapor. *Sayonara, you pitiful sack of crap.*

I was going to have to show some restraint from here on though. Just like before, I needed to take at least one of these killers alive to be interrogated at headquarters. That was my only mission now — to find out why eleven Elites had been murdered and eviscerated.

As I closed in behind the next target, he banked suddenly into a sharp right turn. In fact, he leaned the bike almost horizontally, then brought it back out and whipped into a dark alley. This one was very good, a superior athlete and rider.

The gap was too narrow for my car, but I had another idea. He wouldn't be breaking any motorbike speed limits on these narrow, twisty side streets, after all.

So I screeched to a halt.

"Take over," I snapped to the pilot, popping open the hatch and vaulting out.

"Be careful, Hays," Elle called after me.

How about that. *She'd never used my first name before.* Should that make me extra cautious? Was I in worse danger than I thought?

Chapter 17

I HIT THE ground running, and I mean *running very fast.* I estimated the fleeing rider's distance at thirty-seven yards and his bike's speed at forty-one miles per hour. I could more than match that on foot.

The alley was an unlit black hole of warm, heavy stench that fouled my nostrils, but my night vision picked out every detail, right down to the sweat beading on the skunk's neck, just below his crimson and black helmet.

Within three seconds I'd reached my top foot speed of nearly fifty. By now I was using ten-yard strides. It was almost like flying—my feet barely touching down before I was gone again.

I realized now that I was fully in the human

slum as I stretched to dodge a pile of sludgy food scraps covered in maggots, and a microsyringe and bloody bandages from a hyper-meth junkie. Then I whirled up in a horizontal twist, bounded off the side of a building, and barely cleared a row of overflowing Dumpsters. These humans were absolutely disgusting.

I almost screamed with the sheer, glorious power of the chase. My muscles tensed and sprang like flexing steel bands, the wind rushed past my ears and through my hair, and my teeth clenched in anticipation as I closed the gap on the fleeing killer, hopefully the gang's leader.

A few more seconds and he'd be *mine*—my captive, mine to interrogate.

Then, just as I leaped at him, the sonofabitch yanked his front wheel completely off the ground and bounced up onto a stack of rotting containers. *What in hell?* He used the containers like a springboard to hop over the waist-high wall of an old-style parking garage.

I sailed on past, landed with both heels digging in, spun around, and dove back into the garage after him.

It was so low-ceilinged and full of pilasters

and parked vehicles that my own agility was impaired—I couldn't jump, only run in a crouch over the car tops.

Thump, thump, thump, thump, thump...

He'd started pulling away from me again, racing furiously up the circling ramp. By the time I got to the ramp myself, he'd already reached the third level.

He would find himself trapped on the roof, ten stories up—but what if a getaway pod was waiting for him there?

This was some impressive skunk.

I flew past the ramp, back outside to a corner of the garage, and used every ounce of my strength to spring up twenty feet or so and grip a third-story ledge. Then I swung my feet up under me and leaped another two levels, bounding along the sheer concrete face like a jungle spider chasing an ant. No human could do that—and not many Elites, either. But I wanted this killer badly!

He kept on climbing, and he couldn't see me—probably thought I'd given up. We got to the roof at nearly the same instant. *Big surprise, my smelly friend. Just me and you and the twinkling stars up here!*

This time there was no low ceiling to slow me down. The bike burst into sight up the ramp, moving so fast it actually left the floor in a long arcing jump.

I caught the bastard at its midpoint, slamming into the rider like a cannonball. We landed, twisting and skidding, with my forearm locked around his throat so tight it cracked apart the chin guard of his helmet.

But *damn* if this bastard didn't manage to hang on to the throttle and keep going, racing straight for the outer ledge.

I clung to his back, choking him and wrestling to dump the bike and flip it over, to flip *him*.

My weight tipped us some and started us sliding broadside — but the wheels hit a parking curb and we flipped almost straight up into the air. We were still going so fast the momentum shot us right out over the ledge.

Then we were plunging downward — ten stories to the pavement below.

There, in all probability, we would both die.

Chapter 18

THE NEXT FEW seconds were the longest of my life. I was truly flying, twisting and turning in blissful weightlessness, helpless yet absolutely free.

But a harsh, hate-filled noise interrupted the thought, pushing it away and sucking me back to—

The motorcycle rider was trying to twist himself around so that he could land on top of me—maybe I'd absorb enough impact for him to survive the fall.

Not going to happen! I would have yelled, if there'd been enough time to form the words.

But I did hook my leg tightly behind his. Then I threw my shoulders back and away from him, causing our tangled bodies to shift in the ever-louder, whistling—now *screaming*—air.

For those few seconds, I had been watching the pavement below. Now I saw everything at once—bricks, glass, the side of a building blurring like the view out a train window as it plunges into a tunnel…

The stinging air was pulling, ripping at my hair, my clothes, my lips, my eyelids…and then—

The murderer skunk hit the ground first. I smashed into his body like a pile of lumber landing on a sack of rotten fruit.

And then—nothing at all.

Short circuit?

Death?

I had no idea.

Chapter 19

IN MY FIRST blurred instants of consciousness, before I could even open my eyes, I was somewhat aware of movement—and also that I was floating along flat on my back.

Next came a sharp, clean smell. Antiseptic.

I was in a hospital!

The murmur of voices chattering all around me began to come clear.

One was a woman's, soft, concerned, and very familiar—*Lizbeth.*

Another—a man's, deep voiced and commanding. That would be Jax Moore, the Agency chief, my boss. Lizbeth's boss as well.

There were others, but I didn't recognize any of them at this point.

I realized I must be in New Lake City Hospital, the finest Elite medical facility in the world. I opened my eyes and saw that the other voices belonged to the personnel who were hurrying me on a gurney down a shockingly bright hallway. And to several other people accompanying us— all high-level Elites—some of whom I'd seen earlier at the president's inauguration party.

It appeared that I was enjoying a taste of fame and celebrity. Lucky thing I was still wearing my tux—or, at least, what was left of it.

"Hays," Lizbeth gasped as my eyes fluttered, her lovely face leaning close. "How do you feel, my darling?"

"Never better," I mumbled.

The truth was, I hurt horribly all over, and the constant, astounding pain was getting worse fast. I'd been badly injured before, a number of times, but never in a way I couldn't handle—nothing like this present, unbearable agony.

Of course, I'd never fallen ten stories before. Two or three, sure. Even four once...but ten was clearly more than the doctor, or doctors, ordered.

"What happened to the motorcycle rider?" I

said through clenched teeth. "That killer scum? The skunk?"

"They're scooping him up with shovels," Moore growled at my side.

"Damn! I was trying to keep him alive."

"We know—you gave it a hell of a shot. Now shut up and take it easy, we're almost at the OR. You need some parts replaced, buddy."

Chapter 20

I RELAXED AND managed to give Lizbeth maybe a quarter of a smile. I knew I was in the best possible hands and that Elite medicine had reached a point where I could be good as new — hopefully within a week or two.

But the damn pain was getting worse, and I was weakening in a way I'd never felt before — like the very life was ebbing out of me.

Was that possible — could I be dying? And no one would tell me? Not even Lizbeth? I didn't want to die, especially not so suddenly.

I managed to whisper, "Love you, Jinx. Love the kids."

And she, "Love you, Hays. More than anything in this world. Hang on, sweetheart."

Then the operating room doors swung open and I saw lots of lights. Hospital attendants pushed me inside, then lifted me from the gurney to the table. There, masked, gowned surgeons were already waiting with ultraprecise, computer-moderated surgical tools.

"No time to lose with him," one of them said grimly. "He's on his way out."

Dammit, I didn't need to hear that.

With swift precision, the medical experts adjusted the overhead lights, hooked me up to the banks of monitors and machines, and deftly slid a catheter into my arm. The blessed sedative relief started flowing through my veins, soothing the fiery ache of shrieking nerves.

As I began to slip over the edge of oblivion, I felt the pressure, although no pain, of a laser scalpel opening up my torso.

Then I must have gone into another dream.

Faint and far away, I heard these incredible words:

"My God, look at that! You see that line? That's scar tissue. He's had some sort of surgery here. I think the skin's been grafted. You see how the follicles are different over here from over here? . . .

84

"Look here, underneath...It looks like... Holy shit! You see that?...You see what that is? *That's the remains of a navel cavity!* This guy used to have a belly button! Hays Baker is no Elite.

"He's *human*. This man is a skunk."

Book Two

THE SECRET LIFE OF SKUNKS

Chapter 21

I WAS BEING chased by commandos and trained wildcats. If the cats got to me first, I'd be torn to pieces.

On and on I ran through a murky landscape, the color of dark blood, with the ground endlessly collapsing beneath me and my leaden legs scrambling desperately to stay ahead of God only knows what kind of danger.

The strength I had always depended on was gone—I was weak, helpless, someone who didn't matter anymore, someone who couldn't fight back.

Shadowy terrors clutched at me, and everywhere I turned, hateful faces loomed close, screeching those awful words I imagined I'd heard:

He's human.

The worst thing by far was the terrible shame of the words.

This man is a skunk.

I could feel the wildcats now—so close—and hear the sound they made, like a high-pitched drill.

Chapter 22

I HAD NO idea how long my horrible fugue state lasted, but I finally woke soaked in my own sweat. I must have been thrashing terribly because the bedding was twisted around me like restraints.

Then I realized it wasn't bedding at all; it *was* restraints. I was being held captive for some insane reason that I couldn't comprehend.

Did someone think I might harm myself? Why would I do that?

Faces above me blurred in and out—from dream to reality—until they solidified, glaring down. Not wildcats. One was my partner, Owen McGill, and the other my boss, Jax Moore— except there was no mistaking them for old friends now.

For the first time, I noticed how cold-eyed and thin-lipped Jax Moore's handsome face was, and how McGill's macho, chiseled jaw could have a brutal, almost mechanical look to it. Elites could certainly appear that way, more machine than man.

"Well, well, our traitorous skunk's awake," Moore said, wrinkling his nose as if I were offal he'd accidentally stepped in. "How are you feeling, Hays? We haven't given you anything for the pain. Why should we?"

McGill glowered with outright hatred. "When I think about how I fucking trusted you all these years. The deceit you showed is astonishing."

He leaned close—and then Owen McGill spat in my face. That ended any remaining hope that I might still be dreaming. The sentiment hurt and the spit shamed, but it also pissed me off, big-time.

"What the hell are you saying?" I yelled, struggling to break free. "Have you both gone crazy?"

"There's nobody crazy here," Moore said grimly. "Just two honest cops—and a dirty traitor who will soon be facing the slow death."

"I'll say it again: *Are you crazy?* I'm the best

agent you've ever had! How could I be human? How could that possibly make sense to either of you? Somebody's tricked us! This is a setup!"

"I don't know who you're working with, *skunk,* but we're going to find out in a hurry. You sick bastard."

"Lizbeth!" I raised my voice suddenly. Where was she? Were they holding her too? "What have you done with my wife? And my girls?"

Moore very coolly replied, "Lizbeth and the poor girls are in a safe place. She fainted in my arms when she found out the truth. Then she went home and tried to scrub her skin off— because she had touched you.

"And your daughters…they'll have to go to a new school to try and escape the stigma and shame. Didn't you ever think about what this would do to them? What kind of monster are you?"

Moore stared coldly at me while his words sank in. My wife, my beloved partner in life, she was going along with this? And what would happen to April and Chloe? I didn't want them hurt by vicious accusations against me, no matter how ridiculous and untrue.

"I don't know how you managed to pull this extensive masquerade off, Baker, but we're going to find out." Moore continued his rant. "The doctors want to watch you one more night to make sure you're strong enough for a full interrogation. Then you're coming with us, and believe me, you're going to tell us everything you ever did, from the minute you were born."

Having said that, Moore lit up one of his famous cigars, his *victory* cigars.

"And if you make it through the interrogation, you can guess what's coming next," McGill sneered. "A very slow death. It could take...years."

That's when McGill reared back and punched me hard in the face. The sudden pain made me feel like my skull had been split.

"That'll have to do for now," he growled. "There's plenty more where that came from. Trust me on it. I can't wait to break every bone in your body, skunk."

They turned and stalked out of the room, leaving me rigid with horror, my face aching. I'd seen humans interrogated by Elite experts— reduced to lumps of screaming, gibbering flesh. But that was nothing compared to what McGill promised would come next: *slow death,* a fatal interrogation technique first used by humans during their brutal Terrorist Wars and later perfected by Elites.

I heard Jax Moore bark at some subordinate agents out in the hall: "No mistakes. Keep a close eye on him—he may be human, but he's a slick, dangerous sonofabitch. Remember, he's had augmentations. Probably why he was able to fool us for so long."

My head was pounding with so many questions. I *had* to be an Elite—no human could do the things I could. "Augmentations" couldn't possibly cover it. I mean if humans could be made to perform like top Elites...then why had it never happened before? Even the way my body was healing—didn't that prove something? I was sore, incredibly sore, even in places I hadn't known existed, but everything worked, including my adrenal glands—*I felt like a river gone wild with spring rains.*

But I shoved all that to the back of my brain. The only thing that mattered right now was getting out of here. But how could I? The Agency believed I was a traitor.

I tested the restraints. A metal-enforced jacket bound my upper body and held my arms tightly across my chest. Shackles pinned my wrists and ankles to the bed frame. They were too strong even for me... the world's strongest *human*, right?

Right.

Chapter 23

THIS WAS THE finest hospital in the world—and long ago I had learned this axiom from my mother and father: greatest strength is also greatest weakness.

How could I work with that? There had to be a way out of this. But what was it? What could I do now?

Greatest strength is greatest weakness, I repeated over and over in my head.

Late that night, the highly sensitive cardio monitor near my bed let out a sudden *bleep.* The steady rhythmic line on the screen jumped along with the sound.

A second later it bleeped again, then started

95

into a rapid-fire alarm pattern, while the line leaped in erratic peaks.

A guard stepped into the room — his face hard and wary. Not a shred of sympathy.

"What's going on here?" he barked.

"My heart," I gasped. "Racing like crazy. Won't stop. Feels like it's going to explode."

The guard looked at the cardio monitor, then didn't waste any time — he wheeled around and ordered his partner, "Get the doctors the hell in here! Do it. Now. He's having a heart attack — a big one!"

That was one thing I had in my favor. They wanted me alive, not dead; they had questions that needed answering... about how I got to be me.

Greatest strength is greatest weakness. This was the most efficient hospital in the world — they weren't going to let me die.

I revved my heart rate even higher than the 300 beats per minute I'd already reached. I was pushing 350 when the team of emergency medical personnel burst into the room.

I writhed and grimaced in fake agony, though I actually was in pain. "Can't... breathe," I moaned. "There's an elephant on my chest. Help me! Please!"

Chapter 24

"WHAT THE HELL happened?" one of the doctors yelled at his staff. "You've been monitoring him from central control. The skunk was doing fine five minutes ago."

"Don't ask me—I never wasted any time learning medicine for skunks," another doc said. "We'd better get him out of that jacket though. Take him to a trauma room. He's up to three sixty!"

"Whoa, no you don't," one of the guards said and stepped in. "Our orders are not to let Hays Baker leave the room for any reason. That's not happening. Unless he's in a body bag."

"He's about to stop breathing for good. How's that for a reason?" the lead doctor snapped. "You can explain it to your boss, unless you'd rather explain that you're the one who killed him. *Now get out of our way. He's dying!*"

Reluctantly, the guard stepped back.

Next, a pair of burly orderlies wheeled a gurney alongside my bed. They started to release the restraints.

I had never thought I would harm another Elite. But I'd never had Elites threatening to put me to a slow death either.

I kept up the act, but my muscles were tensed and ready to spring. The instant the shackles were unsnapped and the metal jacket pulled from my arms, I reared straight up out of the bed. I punched the nearest orderly and felt his nose break against my fist. He stumbled back in pain. I caught the second orderly with a chop across the neck, trying not to hurt him too badly. I was also careful to keep the orderlies between myself and the guards' guns.

The Elite doctors were rooted in shock. I pushed them aside and went for the guards, who were already clawing for their pistols. Fortunately, the room was full of equipment, including several monitors on stands.

As I lunged forward, I wrenched one free and swung it like a mace. I took out both guards before they could administer a "fast death" with their guns.

Alarms were shrieking and strobes were flashing all over the building by now. I could hear footsteps pounding down the hallway.

I grabbed a doctor by the neck—the one who'd never wasted his time learning human medicine—and held him in front of me as a shield.

"One more step and I start throwing around his body parts," I yelled at the approaching security team. "And, yes, I'm completely serious about it, and I'm capable. I'm human, right?"

I backed down the hallway to where it turned. I swung the doctor horizontally, then I sprinted toward the front of the building. Now I was using him like a battering ram to crash through everything and everyone in my way.

Carts went flying, gurneys were overturned, wide-eyed, shrieking nurses leaped back against the walls to avoid being trampled.

Still holding on to my screeching hostage, I bounded down an escalator to the lower level.

Next, I burst into the cafeteria's kitchen, where blank-faced robot workers tended the huge, metallic complex, churning out no-cal grub that was also virtually no-taste.

As I raced through, I dropped the doc into a bin of scraps. I caught a glimpse of his bulging-eyed face as he flopped around in the rank garbage.

"That'll teach you to call me a skunk," I told him.

Then I charged out through a loading-dock door into an alley—and, hopefully, the freedom of the night.

Unfortunately, I thought, *maybe I am a skunk*.

Chapter 25

THE COOL, FRESH night air quickly filled my lungs and began to dry the fevered hospital sweat off my skin. Adrenaline was keeping the pain at bay, and running was stretching and loosening my traumatized body.

Before long, I was pounding along the pavement at close to my top speed, fifty miles an hour.

I had to see my daughters and my wife— hold them in my arms, tell them I loved them, try to explain that whatever wicked stories they might hear weren't true. Or, at least, that there had to be some reasonable explanation for the mix-up.

No matter what else, I wasn't a traitor. That much I was certain of.

James Patterson

Our apartment wasn't far from the hospital; I reached the building in less than ten minutes.

Suddenly, I was very nervous and apprehensive.

I paused to listen for sounds of pursuit, but there was nothing out of the ordinary. Not so far, anyway. The side-door entrance recognized my bioprint and opened on contact. The police probably figured this would be the last place I'd go right now. I hoped so.

Was it possible that Lizbeth had turned on me as totally as Jax Moore said she had? Or was he lying—another part of this insanity? But why would he lie to me?

This time, when Metallico answered the apartment door, there was no robo-rap music playing, or sounds of any kind. The place felt empty. The air smelled strongly of antiseptic, and there were cleaning materials left out all over the living room.

"Hello, Hays," Metallico said. "I'm afraid I can't invite you in. Sorry about that."

His tone was flat and neutral, and he seemed downright stiff—like an ordinary android instead of his usual sassy self.

"This is my house. You work here. What do

you mean you can't invite me in?"

"The apartment is being decontaminated."

"Where are they?" I demanded. "Lizbeth? The girls? I need to know. Right now, Metallico! I'm not in the mood for games."

"I'm not at liberty to say. That's final."

I groaned. This was going nowhere fast, and I was pretty sure this unfaithful robot had already sounded the emergency alarm. Indeed, my hearing picked up the sound of fast-approaching airborne cars—and a couple more vehicles stopping on the streets below. I suppose I should have expected as much.

I rammed the heel of my hand into the robot's silicone chest, sending him spinning across the room. Metallico crashed into a wall with a bright flash as his circuits collapsed and shorted him out.

"Take that, you treacherous vacuum cleaner!" I said, standing over his crumpled body.

Next, I peeled the silicone skin off the back of his bulb-shaped head. I quickly removed his short-term-memory chip, grabbed my backup PDA from the drawer in the desk in the hall, and dumped the chip's data into it.

"Grandmère," I said, sighing. Of course. Lizbeth had taken the kids to her mother's house in the suburbs. Where else?

Grandmère was an aging, but still beautiful, lady with an icy charm and a keen sense of social class. Only the best of the Elites were good enough for her.

Once upon a time, that had meant me, but no more. And, probably, never again.

Dammit though, I missed my family. *Didn't that alone prove I was Elite?*

Chapter 26

NO TIME FOR such sentimentality. The Agency commandos would be up here in seconds, heavily armed, ready to kill me if they had to. I was fairly certain the luxury building was already surrounded. So I ran to the back of the apartment and threw open the balcony door. Sure enough, police vehicles were already circling in the air and barricading escape routes on the ground. They wanted me — *badly.*

Spotlights flared suddenly. A voice boomed, "Stop where you are, Hays Baker! Down on your belly and spread your arms and legs!"

I'd spent time on the other side of those spotlights, and I knew the weapons that went with them — stun guns that would paralyze me *if* they were determined to keep me alive. Or lasers that would turn me into a six-foot-two cinder.

Question was—did they want to keep up this charade of pretending I was a skunk who needed to be brought in and interrogated?

I dove sideways to the neighboring balcony, twenty yards away, caught its lower rim, and swung myself down to the floor below.

The searchlights followed, and then bursts of laser fire hissed around me.

Well, *that* question was answered anyway. I was obviously wanted—dead or alive.

I went from balcony to balcony, flipping and twisting like a monkey dodging poison darts. Only the poison darts were traveling at the speed of light and punching three-inch-wide gashes in the concrete walls. Also, if I'd actually been a monkey, I'd have already lost my tail—one of the blasts came so close that it set the trailing edge of my hospital gown on fire.

I didn't bother swatting it out. No time for that. Instead, I plunged headfirst toward the dark, roiling surface of the lake below. A blitz of searchlights and laser flashes followed me, but I somehow sliced into the cold water.

One good thing to be said for a 110-foot dive from a high-rise into a North American lake in the early summer: the freezing cold water quickly takes your attention away from the sting of slamming into the lake's surface.

It was hard to hold my breath and think straight when all I wanted to do was scream. But I stayed underwater, knowing that cover meant survival.

My brain was racing faster than my body now. What next? Normally, I could hold my breath for several minutes, but how far would I be able to swim in that time? *Well, let's see!*

I swam straight for the opposite shore — my strokes actually getting stronger — and finally ended up in a partially submerged culvert. The storm sewer it connected to ran up under the Esplanade, an eight-lane highway that bordered the lake.

I entered the first manhole shaft I came to, climbed furiously up, and came out in the middle of a landscaped median full of tulips, roses, exotic grasses, and hybrid cherry trees in full bloom.

The city's ground traffic was heavy as usual, moving at a crawl — about thirty-five miles per hour.

It was just slow enough for me to sprint after the most anonymous-looking service vehicle I saw, grab hold of its rear bumper, then tuck myself down between the rear wheels, hopefully hidden from overhead police scanners.

In a matter of a few seconds, I had disappeared into the flood of vehicles flowing in and out of New Lake City.

As in the theme song from that old movie — one of the James Bond films, I believe — "nobody does it better."

Chapter 27

STILL PLAYING THE superhero in my head—it just might help me survive—I jumped off the service vehicle as it slowed for its destination, a distribution center on the edges of an infamous human slum on the south side of town. I smelled the humans before I actually saw one. No wonder they were called skunks.

Humans aren't the most fashion-savvy creatures on the planet, but even so, I figured I would stand out in my singed hospital gown. To avoid attracting too much attention, I stayed in alleyways and shadows, scouting for food, shelter, and, yes, clothes to replace the johnny.

It was a depressingly poor and bombed-out area of town, and there weren't a lot of inviting spaces around. Mostly it was a long row of metal-sided buildings, shuttered loading docks, and gritty, litter-strewed sidewalks.

I'd gone maybe a half mile in the direction of what looked to be a human neighborhood when I rounded a corner and saw a group of jeering Betas—named so by Elite sociologists because they behaved like lawless young male wolves, living lives of opportunistic violence on the edge of the pack. The dangerous human thugs were armed with knives and clubs and were clearly not on their way to help out at an area soup kitchen.

They'd surrounded a girl—she couldn't have been much more than sixteen years old, and she looked very pregnant. As they shoved her back and forth, her pale, tattered skirt billowed up around her waist. She was screaming at the top of her voice: "Nooo, my baby!"

It was against my Agency training to put myself at risk for a human, but the girl was clearly in trouble. I had to help her if I possibly could. But could I?

"Nice dress, man," said the lead Beta as I approached the punks.

His friends stopped molesting the girl long

enough to size me up and then pull a couple of knives from their belts.

"See anything you like?" I offered up a human-style wisecrack. "Maybe I do."

"Watch it, pretty boy," said the leader, a bull-shouldered hulk with a scarred face and a broken nose.

"Aren't you going to ask me to dance?" I said.

"We'll dance with you all right—till you're bleedin' out of places you've never bleeded before."

"Sounds like fun," I told him. "Will it hurt? I like pain."

His buddies had stepped away from the terrified girl and were gathering around me now. The girl took off running down a nearby alleyway. Not even so much as a thank-you.

"Yeah," the lead trog went on, clearly pleased with himself. "Why don't we do some *slam*-dancing? We stand in a circle like this, and you get *slammed*."

"Or," I said, not to be outdone in my knowledge of retro human dances, "we could *break*-dance. You know, you try to lay a hand on me, and I *break* your ugly heads?"

His grin widened and then disappeared into an expression of stone-cold seriousness. "Kill 'im, boys. Rip 'im up."

It so happened that I was already having a very bad day and had some serious aggression to work out. In fact, the hardest part would be checking my fury so that I didn't overdo it and end up coming out of this fight without any usable clothes from this rat pack.

Of course, *usable* is a relative term. After I'd won the street fight—in under a minute—and stripped a couple of the skunks' semiconscious bodies, I almost decided to stick with my hospital gown. Their pants, boots, shirts, and jackets smelled *that* bad.

At first I was convinced the clothes achieved what I wanted: they made me look—and smell—just like another Beta. But as I buckled up my pants, I realized somebody wasn't entirely buying the costume. Footsteps were coming up behind me lickety-split. *Now what?*

I took a breath and got ready for another fight.

It was just the young girl though, and she was very pregnant indeed. Poor thing.

Chapter 28

NORMALLY, I DESPISED sentimentality—except when it came to Lizbeth and my girls—but I found that I couldn't help myself. Maybe my own recent circumstances were teaching me some compassion. I certainly hoped not.

The girl's teeth were broken and decayed, and her skin pockmarked by some childhood disease, probably treatable at the time. Sad to say, but hospitals and other medical care for the humans were substandard at best. It was a policy I didn't approve of, but the president had never asked my opinion on the subject.

"Can't b-believe you got 'em *all*," she stammered, with the slangy inflection of so many humans in these slums. "How'd ya do it?"

"Just dumb luck, I suppose. But I'm sure there are others lurking around. You should go someplace safe. Don't depend on me, girl."

She laughed, exposing several more infected teeth. "Safe? In Beta-Town? You're not from around here, are ya?"

"Yeah, I guess you could say that."

"Come with me," she said. "Going to storm hard soon. I got a place."

She was right about the weather. The sultry air was thickening and held the promise of rain, and this was the time of year that flash floods were common. I was bone tired too — my body wasn't through with its healing.

Still, I was about to politely decline her offer when she moaned in pain and doubled over, clutching her swollen belly. Then she started to fall.

I caught the girl in my arms and eased her down to the ground. After a minute, her face smoothed out. Actually, the face was rather pretty, so long as she kept her mouth closed.

"When's the baby due?" I asked.

"Few weeks yet. But those Betas, they punched me here." She clasped her hands tighter around her stomach, cradling what was inside.

I let out a sigh. "How far is your place?" I asked.

"Not far. I'll show you. Don't be afraid—you can trust me."

As I scooped her up in my arms, I felt wetness drenching the back of her thin skirt.

Good Lord, the girl was bleeding badly. Her baby could die.

Chapter 29

SHE TOLD ME her name as we hurried along to her place. It was Shanna. I asked a few harmless questions, trying to keep her mind off the pain—and the blood—as best I could.

Turns out, Shanna had been on her own since she was ten, living with various destitute groups of humans until Betas, disease, or hunger forced her to move on. Shanna didn't know where she'd been born, who her parents were, or even who her baby's father was. She said that she was a "Southerner" and a "Baptist" and a "Bible-thumper," none of which meant anything to me.

"How old are you, Shanna?" I finally had to ask.

"Fourteen," she told me. "I'm fourteen. Old enough."

As we went farther into the human neighborhood, the air became rank with the sickly sweet stink of rot. All manner of insects buzzed, fluttered, and scurried around Shanna and me. I was coming to realize that I'd taken several comforts of Elite life completely for granted. Also, that I'd given almost no thought to the terrible living conditions of humans. This place was unendurable.

"Here," Shanna said. She weakly raised a hand to point down an alley that had patches of high weeds thrusting up through its cracked concrete.

As we entered the alley, the voice of a lookout shouted, "*Betas!* Two of 'em."

I heard fast shuffling, like a pack of huge animals scurrying closer to us.

I bent to set Shanna down so I could fight them off.

"It's OK," she managed to call out. "He helped me. He's a good man!"

The shuffling sounds stopped. Then, pale faces came slowly into sight, peering out of a dark building at the alley's far end. There could have been a dozen of them, or twice that many. They were hard to tell apart—all so thin and furtive.

Even the very young ones radiated extreme fear and suffering of the sort I had never encountered before.

"It's a trick! Why would a Beta help ya?" a tall woman demanded, stepping forward defiantly. She was older, but far from infirm, and gave off a sense of intelligence and self-possession that I was surprised to see in this slum.

"Oh, I'm not a Beta—I just borrowed some clothes...after I fought a few of them," I said. "Look here, Shanna's in a bad way. She's bleeding a lot. Where do you want me to take her?"

"He's telling the truth. I think the baby's coming, Corliss," Shanna said in a trembling voice. Then, very softly, the girl started to cry like, well, a little girl.

Concern spread across the older woman's face. "This way," she said, and led us quickly into a small room in a run-down warehouse. There was a mattress of rags on the floor and a table covered with rancid food scraps. Human photographs were pinned on the walls.

I'd studied the biological phenomenon of human birth, even seen footage of it on the Cybernet, but I'd never witnessed it in person.

Chloe and April—as with all Elite babies—
were born in synthetic wombs in government-
regulated natal centers.

The difference was one of the most funda-
mental between humans and Elites.

Or so I believed at the time.

Chapter 30

HOW STRANGE IT was—being among these humans, pretending to be one of them.

After I settled Shanna on the mattress, she began to tell her friends what had happened with the Betas, speaking haltingly in a human street dialect I could barely follow.

Their looks toward me became cautiously admiring. "How can we repay you?" Corliss finally asked.

"I just need to rest awhile. That's thanks enough," I said. "I'll be on my way soon."

"Stay here as long as you wish," said Corliss. "You're a friend now. And I can see you've been injured yourself."

"I'll be fine. Honestly."

I walked farther back into the building—an abandoned warehouse with the doors and windows long since gone. There was no electricity, no running water, but at least it was shelter from the rain and wind that had started outside—not to mention any Elite satellites and drones that might be scanning the city for signs of me.

I stepped into a large room nearby and found ragged children huddled there—playing with, of all things, Jessica and Jacob dolls. It seemed ironic that these street urchins had been able to steal the most sought-after toys of the season—but that wasn't what bothered me. When I really thought about it, there was something just *wrong* about dolls that acted out everything we did… but were only a foot or so tall. It was just weird to me. Also, dolls *used* to be about children exercising their imaginations, about real *play*. How were children going to exercise their minds if the dolls did the playing by themselves?

"Those things aren't good for you," I told the kids. "They'll rot your brains."

"If you're so smart, what are you doing *here*?" one of them snapped back.

The others giggled and muttered in their coarse slang, insulting me. It was disturbing to see people so hard-edged at such a young age. No doubt some of them would go on to become Betas—if they survived that long.

But I was actually heartened by the kids' smart-aleck reaction. There was surprising verve, an underlying vitality, in this human ghetto. The skunks were a little more clever, and more rational, than I'd formerly believed. I was also detecting kindness alongside the cruelty, passion within the desperation.

Strains of music drifted through the air—and I caught, in the shadows, the whispering, giggling sounds of lovemaking.

I finally found a quiet corner to settle in. I needed to rest and regenerate. A few minutes later, Corliss brought me a basket of food—a half loaf of fresh bread, along with scraps of cheese and vegetables. My stomach growled like an animal's. I couldn't remember ever being so hungry, and though part of me shuddered at the thought of eating nutritionally unbalanced, germy, possibly toxin-laden human food, my mouth watered at the sight and smell of it.

I took a couple of tentative chews and then began tearing into what was my breakfast, lunch, and dinner of the day.

But simply eating their food didn't make me one of them. Every time the words *he's human* resurfaced in my mind, I shuddered and shook my head in confusion. What had happened to me, and to my family? I couldn't be human—I *wasn't*.

And that's when I heard Shanna's blood-curdling screams.

Chapter 31

WHY DID I feel responsible for this girl? Why should I?

Still, I rushed down the hallway, hoping it wasn't Betas attacking or, worse, the city police looking for me.

But it was just Shanna—in labor. The baby was coming already, probably prematurely.

The others had dragged her rag mattress next to an old iron storage rack. Her small bare feet were braced against the uprights.

Some delivery room. Filthy, no proper instruments, no drugs to ease the girl's pain.

Corliss, looking nervous and worried, was kneeling between Shanna's thighs.

"Good, we need someone strong," Corliss said

as she saw me enter the room. "Hold her hands." Then she added, "Do you have a name?"

"It's Hays," I said.

"All right, Hays, hold this poor girl down. Hold her good! She's in for a world of pain."

So I crouched behind Shanna's head and took hold of her. The girl's fingers tightened around my wrists, her nails digging in, drawing blood. And then she began to scream again— and to curse Corliss, then me, and, finally, life itself.

Corliss patiently soothed and coaxed the girl. "You have to push like a madwoman, hon," she kept saying. "I know how bad it hurts, but you have to push so hard. Come on. Push hard, dear. It'll be over soon. I promise. *Push*."

"You're lying! You're all liars! Assholes!"

On and on like that.

Finally, though, the human baby's head started to appear. This was unbelievable to me. It almost seemed like a miracle.

"*Push!*" Corliss urged. "The baby's crowning! Push! You're almost there. I promise you, Shanna. *I'm not lying this time!*"

The girl's screams and grunts continued—

until quite suddenly, a little boy, slick with blood, slipped out into Corliss's waiting hands.

Corliss raised and examined the infant carefully, even lovingly. He was small, but seemed perfectly formed as he kicked his tiny feet and started to wail.

Except for the blood and the umbilical cord running into his belly, he looked just like April and Chloe had when Lizbeth and I had first seen them, fresh from the incubator.

Tiny. Perfect. Heart-stopping.

I let go of Shanna's wrists and stood up. I was sweating, rattled worse than I'd ever been in the line of duty.

My God, that was something—*helping in a human birth.*

I got another unexpected jolt when Corliss brought the baby's belly up close to her face—and *bit* off the umbilical cord.

Smiling, Corliss settled the tiny tyke on Shanna's breasts and kissed the new mom's forehead. "Congratulations, darling," she said. "You did so well. You were brave and you were strong."

There was no reason for me to stay any longer, and I started toward the room's exit.

"Please stay," Shanna said. "You saved me. You saved the baby."

I was startled — not just by her words, but by the intense feelings that rose up in me. I'd never cared about humans. Far from it. But now it struck me that maybe I'd never considered their plight fairly. Why hadn't it seemed possible that there was more to them than what the Cybernet said? Why had I been content to study and enjoy their colorful history, literature, art — their music especially — but dismiss humans themselves as self-destructive animals?

Shanna's imploring eyes brought me back to the moment.

"Look, I have to keep moving," I said. "But" — I hesitated, realizing that I was about to make an insane promise — "I'll come back. I want to see your baby again."

She nodded slowly, and so did Corliss.

Then I did something truly amazing.

I reached down and touched the baby's soft cheek. His eyes were still closed, but his little mouth smiled at me.

"I have to go now," I said. "But thank you — for letting me be part of this."

Chapter 32

I HAD FINALLY figured out something useful. I knew what I had to do now and where I had to go—if I wanted to solve the mystery that had suddenly become my life. It was so obvious.

"I want to buy your car," I said.

The man I was speaking to, a midlevel Elite just about to climb into his sporty Mazda ZX-740 airpod, looked stunned. I probably could have broached the subject more subtly, but I was in a hurry. I was a man with a plan now.

"Huh?" said the man. "I don't want to *sell* you my car."

"Yes, you do. Now come on, I'm in a real bind here. Name your price."

He glanced around quickly, a grasp of the

situation slowly creeping across his face. After walking to the edge of the human slums where Shanna lived, I had hopped on public transit and ridden to a commuter suburb of the city. A place with resplendent green lawns, backyard wave-pools, choreographed fountains, gold-plated driveway gates, and cozy commercial centers with boutiques, spas, high-end jewelers, and cafés that sold cups of organic coffee that cost more than the average human salary. A place, in short, where crime was almost unheard-of.

But the bottom line was that it was six o'clock in the morning, it was drizzling, there was not another soul in sight, and this poor guy was facing someone who looked like a human thug— and who was possibly crazy, or high on wyre.

"I'm not selling you my car. You should leave this neighborhood. *Now,*" he finally said. We were standing outside the only twenty-four-hour establishment in the area, a convenience store.

"Listen," I said, talking fast enough to keep him off balance. "This is the all-environments model, right? Works on-road, off-road, airborne? Can safely dive to one thousand meters underwater? Gull-wing doors? Ultrasonic massage seats? THX six-point-three holographic surround sound? What's the sticker price? Like three twenty? Tell you what, I don't have time to haggle"—I rummaged in the pockets of the pants I'd taken off the Beta and came up with seven dollars and some change—"but I'm a little short of cash right now. So I guess I'll have to borrow some money from you too."

His mouth opened in complete disbelief, but then his face took on a cynical smirk. "This is some kind of joke, right? It has to be a joke."

I stepped forward, gripped his lapels with one hand, and lifted him off his feet.

"No joke," I said. "I'm sorry about this—but I *need* your car. My life depends on it."

Chapter 33

I GOT IN the ZX and quickly overrode the vehicle-identification circuits and security beacons so that the car's computer wouldn't recognize me as an unauthorized driver. "Sorry about this," I called to the poor guy outside. "I *will* pay you back eventually. This really is life or death for me."

The ZX took off in a streak while I settled back in the driver's seat. It flew like a dream and had all sorts of features I hadn't used before—like Level Two Priority Traffic Access, which let me cut right through the city's elaborate air-traffic-control patterns by steering me to the shortest routes available to nonemergency or police vehicles. A total Elite VIP perk.

I stopped at a high-end Toyz store along

the way and came out wearing new clothes: black jeans, a fitted T-shirt, a leather jacket, wraparound shades to hide my face. I had also downloaded some tattoo art at the Toyz Corp iTattoo booth. Like many Elites, I went in for tattoo-zone implants as a teen—one on the back of my neck, another on my right forearm. I can activate either to become visible—or fade back to skin tone—at a moment's notice.

I also purchased an ultrasonic shaver and a tube of EliteMan follicle-activation cream—one quick application and you could instantly grow yourself a fashionable hint of stubble.

Back in the car, I shaved my head—right to the scalp—and quickly gave myself a five o'clock shadow on the chin and cheeks. Then I activated the new tattoo art—a fist-sized tarantula on my forearm, a Harley-Davidson logo on the back of my neck.

Now I looked nothing like the old Hays Baker; I was just another of the wealthy, weekend-warrior civilians you'd expect to see in the Baronville Toyz store, where eleven executives had recently been murdered. That was where I was headed now. I'd made up my mind; I needed one more look at the crime scene where my life had begun to be shattered.

I needed to know *why* my life had been blown to pieces.

There had to be clues I'd overlooked. Also, why had Jax Moore insisted on calling me there, even though it was well outside my area of operations? What had happened to make the in-store witnesses forget everything they'd seen?

Hopefully, I'd learn something soon—because there was the Toyz store, less than a hundred yards straight ahead.

The place where everything had gone all wrong for me, and for my family.

Chapter 34

THAT LAST THOUGHT reminded me of the girls—and suddenly I had another idea, probably my most constructive one so far.

Chloe and April both carried phones to school—and maybe, just maybe, I could talk to them now.

I dialed Chloe's number first, then I couldn't believe it when I actually heard her voice come on the line. *Thank God, it was her!*

"This is Chloe Baker," she said. An odd first line, but it was definitely my baby.

"This is your daddy. Hello, Chloe Baker," I said.

"Daddy, what happened to you? Mommy said you're in trouble—bad trouble. Is that true? It couldn't be, right?"

"Chloe, sweetie, it's just a misunderstanding. I'll be home soon."

There was a silence, which I didn't understand. Chloe tends to talk and talk.

"Chloe? *Chloe?* What's the matter? Something is — I can tell —"

Chloe blurted out, *"Daddy, the police are listening! The police are at my school!"*

Then she clicked off the phone.

Talk about a heartbreaking call.

But why did I feel things so deeply?

Like a human would?

Chapter 35

I KNEW I'D better hurry—the police could be here soon. It was almost surreal being back at the murder scene, especially since the Agency and city police were now searching for me. I strained to keep my vitals in check so that I wouldn't set off any biometric-profile monitors in the Toyz store, but my nerves weren't helped any by having to go past the window display of Jessica and Jacob dolls. They were strutting around like they owned that little world.

The customers inside Toyz were the same mix of Elites and the occasional upper-level humans I'd seen here the other night.

Almost immediately, I recognized a face—the pretty Elite woman I'd first interviewed, the one who said she'd been standing right next to two of the victims but hadn't actually witnessed the murders.

How could she bear to come back here so soon after that hideous crime, and then wander around clothes and baubles, shopping as if nothing had happened? Was she that callous? Or had something mysterious happened to her? If so, what was it? *I needed to find out why nobody had seen eleven murders.*

The woman was talking to a salesclerk, so I'd have to wait for a chance to pull her aside. That wasn't good—I wanted to get out of here *now*.

Meantime, there were security personnel posted all around the lobby floor. I couldn't just stand there looking like a police investigator. So I walked to the nearest bank of SimStims and picked out a diversion that was consistent with my general appearance.

"Rock the Cosmos!" the display flashed, throbbing with the loud treble and hammering bass of the latest fad, "sycho" music.

I set the timer for ninety seconds and slipped on the helmet.

And man, did I ever rock! I was strutting around

the huge stage, surrounded by a crowd that went on as far as I could see—a hundred thousand fans at least. They were waving their arms and dancing to the wild pulse of the music—and it was all about me. I was the center of attention, the target of all the screaming and adoration! Not so bad, I had to admit. Certainly better than being chased around by the police and the Agency.

One of the huge amplifiers suddenly exploded, showering the spectators, and me, with debris. The crowd cheered louder, danced even closer to the stage, screamed the lyrics along with my vocals—

Abruptly, the concert was gone—and I was standing alone in the sound booth.

"Presented by Toyz Corporation," a blinking message stated. "We hope you enjoyed—"

I wheeled around, tugging off the helmet. Honestly, I had been lost in the moment!

Then I looked for the witness.

It was a little disorienting, and dizzying, what you experienced after a SimStim even as brief as that. Could that be good for you? Especially for people who used SimStims as much as ten to fifteen hours a day?

Finally, I spotted the female witness, alone now, moving up an escalator. I managed to catch up to her on the mezzanine floor. I needed to be careful.

"So, did you ever get one of those iSpielberg imagers?" I asked.

She turned and looked at me, slightly confused. "Umm—do I know you?"

"We talked the other night. Don't you remember? After the murders."

"Murders? Oh. Here at the store, right? So terrible. Mindless violence."

"I'm Ben," I said, trying not to show surprise at her detachment. "You? Your name is?"

"It's Chuzie. I'm Chuzie."

"Chuzie, like—"

"Like I'm *choosy* about, well, all sorts of things," she said, looking me up and down, apparently approving of something.

"So what happened? What did you see? The night of the murders?" I asked her.

"Why are you asking *me*? I don't understand. You said you were there too."

"I know. That's the really strange part. I'm having trouble remembering any of it myself."

Chuzie nodded her head several times. Then she frowned, looking confused again. "You know, I had this crazy *dream* about the murders..."

"What happened—in the dream?" I asked, gesturing for her to sit on the edge of an XRBed—a magnetic-field-assisted mattress that exercised your muscles while you slept.

"Well, there were a lot of city cops everywhere. I believe the Agency was here too. And something else I can't quite remember." Her shoulders twitched in a little shiver. "Whatever it was, it was bad."

This was ridiculous. Why would a civilian, an Elite, be going to such lengths to distance herself from the truth?

"Chuzie, people were killed. You were standing right next to them. I saw you. Don't you remember anything?"

She was biting her lower lip furiously, starting to look a little scared. "In the dream there was all of this screaming. Then blood everywhere."

"Did anybody *say* anything? Do you remember any of the faces? The attackers?"

"A human...with a big knife. A machete? He was—he was cutting off someone's *head*. And he said, 'Now we'll find out what you know.'"

Abruptly, she clapped her hands to the sides of her face. "Why are you asking me this? Who are you?"

And then a shrill voice yelled out, "It's *him!* It's Hays Baker. Get him! He's human scum!"

Chapter 36

SPEECHLESS, I LOOKED down to see that one of the Jacob dolls had followed us. He was pointing an accusing finger at me. And then little Jacob said, "You are going to get the *slow death*, big man!"

"Well, better that than the *swift kick*," I said, picking him up and punting him out over the escalator bank. I took some satisfaction in hearing his shrill little scream silence as he smashed through a Perfumone display case—but it was a short-term fix to a much larger problem.

The store's alarms were blaring, security bolts on the doors began slamming shut, and police sirens started to wail in the distance.

"Thanks for your help," I told the Elite woman. "I have to run."

I picked up and heaved a 300- to 400-pound SimStim booth through a window. Then I leaped after it, landing on the street outside in a shower of splintered glass.

"Halt, Hays Baker!" a loud digitized voice boomed somewhere behind me. "We will shoot to kill! Repeat, we will shoot to kill!"

Tell me about it. I took off past the simulation booth, zigzagging my way back to the car.

Minutes later, I was in the ZX and weaving through the streets of New Lake City, keeping the speed down to 180 miles per hour so as not to attract undue attention. I was pretty sure I'd gotten away from the store without the cops spotting me. Even better, I didn't see anyone following now.

At the city's northern outskirts, high-rise buildings and fancy houses gave way to an industrial area filled with long, low warehouses and factories.

As the streets opened into freight-friendly freeways, I jacked my speed up to 300.

It looked like I'd made it one more step on this journey—wherever it was leading.

I set the locator code for my parents' house

and switched the car over to automatic pilot. My folks lived far out in the north country, so the trip would take approximately four hours.

"OK, I need to rest," I said. "May I have a very dry vodka martini? I think I deserve it."

"With pleasure," said the personal-attendant program. Slim, red-fingernail-tipped hands opened the bar compartment and mixed the drink. "What else can I do for you?"

"You know, what I really want is some sleep. Wake me up a few minutes before we get to the south shore of Lake Wabago, will you?"

"Of course. How about a full-body massage to help you relax?" she said, and added, "It's one of my specialties."

"Sounds terrific," I said.

And was it ever. Her fingers started on my neck and shoulders, probing gently into my exceedingly tense muscles. Like all the best robotic massages, this one featured infrared heat radiating from the android's fingertips, soothing body tissue clear down to the bones.

When I finished the martini, I reclined all the way back in the seat and stretched out as far as I could. The attendant's smooth hands unfastened my shirt and started working on my chest.

"I hope you don't mind me saying this, but you've got a great body," she murmured.

"I don't mind," I said. "Most people have been kind of down on me lately."

Sleep, I told myself. *You have to sleep.*

And that's what I did.

Chapter 37

A FEW HOURS later, I was fully alert and back at the wheel. The personal attendant gasped excitedly as I made a sharp left turn and plunged the ZX headfirst into the lake that surrounded the island where my parents lived. Stabilizing fins shot out from the sides of the pod, and the drivetrain instantly disengaged from the wheels and connected to the rear water jets.

"Oooh, I'm so wet," the attendant chirped seductively. This was a sports model after all, a boy's toy.

I loved the car for its performance attributes, if nothing else. I'd already decided that if I survived long enough, I was going to find the guy I'd taken it from and buy it for real.

It glided along smoothly, skirting sunken logs and sending schools of bass and perch darting away. When I was a kid, I'd spent a lot of time up here on the lake with my dad, fishing for walleyed pike, lake trout, even eels, which can be surprisingly delicious when cooked up fresh after the catch.

I hadn't seen my folks much since university — and then I'd become an Agent of Change and married Lizbeth. I loved and respected my parents, but, well, they weren't the easiest people to be around.

I'd always known they were unusual, even odd. Before I was born, they'd invested in the biotech industry and done well. But they decided they wanted a simpler life, so they moved to this faraway, wild north country on the lake. Now they spent their time gardening and tinkering without much connection to society, and they seemed to like it that way. They saw Lizbeth, me, and the kids once a year, and that seemed enough for them, which was strange to me. My parents had always been warm and loving when I was a child.

The ZX shot up out of the water and onto a

pebbly beach, then it snaked through a stretch of thick, tangled forest while tree limbs brushed its roof and windows.

It was late morning now, cloudy and warm, the leaves glistening with dew and the air thick with birdsong. The forest opened into a large clearing—and *there* was the sprawling, old-fashioned house where I'd grown up. Everything looked just the way I remembered it, cedar shingles and all. Even the smell of the pine trees was familiar.

Except that someone I didn't recognize was up on a ladder, working on the roof. It was a woman who had her hair tucked under a painter's cap. She must have been a human my parents had hired to do the chores, although I didn't recall them mentioning it, or ever doing that before. They'd always taken care of the place themselves. Well, they weren't getting any younger, were they? Nobody was.

"So you made it here on your own," the menial worker called as I climbed out of the car. "I'm impressed. You're more resourceful than I would have guessed."

The timbre of her voice registered immediately

in my brain, and it was like I'd been zapped with a Taser—the woman was the leader of the gang of skunks who had attacked Lizbeth and me, *the one who got away.*

Chapter 38

I FOUGHT BACK wild surprise—and then a wave of rage—and managed a frosty smile worthy of my former rank and station at the Agency. *Am I walking into an ambush? Are my parents here—are they even alive?* I wondered, in that order.

"Well, well," I said. "Last time we met, you tried to kill me."

"If I'd tried," she said, putting down a hammer and removing leather work gloves, "you'd be dead."

Was the woman deliberately trying to provoke me? Clearly she and whomever she was working for were a step ahead of me. Maybe several steps. How was that even possible?

"Where are my parents?" I asked as I judged the height of the roof and got ready to leap up there, fight her, and kill her.

"They'll be out in a minute to say hello to their favorite son. Calm down, Hays. No need for you to come up here and try out your fancy commando moves on me."

This time her condescending tone—as if she were soothing an upset child—was a little too much for my nerves.

"Don't tell me to calm down. You're a common killer—a criminal and a skunk."

"I guess by your standards I am. But by most other standards, you're the criminal. How many humans have you killed in your life, Hays Baker?" she shot back. "Or have you lost count? And what does that say about you?"

Just then the front door of the house swung open, and out came my mother. She hurried toward me with a welcoming smile and open arms.

"Hays, darling, it's so wonderful to see you! I'm so happy you're here."

Mom was thinner and noticeably older than the last time I'd been here, but her eyes were more luminous than ever. She looked healthy and spry enough.

"I see you've met Lucy," she said, gesturing up at the roof. But then her eyes were back on me, *her favorite son*. Of course, I was her *only* child.

"What a sight you are," she said, looking me up and down, then clasping me again in her warm embrace. Ah, the feel of her, the scent of her skin, the sound of her voice...I really was home, wasn't I?

She finally stepped back, taking hold of my hands and looking me over again. "But for heaven's sake—what happened to your beautiful hair?"

I ran my hand over my bald head. "It's the new look in the city," I said. Then I asked, "Who is *she*, and why is she here?"

My mother looked deep into my eyes, and then she said, "She's here because she's your sister."

Chapter 39

I IMMEDIATELY SWIVELED my head back and forth from the smart-mouthed criminal—and, perhaps, murderer—up on the roof to my mother. My mom was clearly not under any kind of duress or threat. If anything, I sensed embarrassment coming from her.

"What do you mean, my '*sister*'?" I asked the obvious question.

"We just couldn't tell you about Lucy. It would have been too risky," my father said, stepping out of the house. "It was too important that you accomplish what you've done so well. Become one of them. Become an Elite bastard."

What the hell was going on here?

What was my father talking about? What had

they done? Had my parents played me like some sort of unwitting pawn? Had they purposely set out to make me a traitorous "bastard"? Was I a sleeper agent?

"Come with me. Please, Hays," he said. "Just come. I have something to show you."

I obediently followed him to the outbuilding that he used as a workshop. It was all so very familiar, especially the cloying smell of oil and paint inside.

"Nothing changes, does it?" I muttered. "It's as if I never went away."

"Looks just like what you'd expect from a harmless, bumbling eccentric, right?" my father said, gesturing with his hand at the contents of the musty, cluttered space. Several tables were covered with a jumble of random electronic gadgetry. None of it seemed to point to any unified purpose or goal.

"That's a good way to put it," I agreed. Like most young kids, I had never paid too much attention to what my parents actually *did* in their work.

In my human-history studies at university, I'd come across countless descriptions of the "hippie" movement of the 1960s. Richard Brautigan, Tom Wolfe, Ken Kesey, a movie called *Woodstock*. I soon realized that my parents—with their off-the-grid, tuned-out-of-the-mainstream lifestyle—bore more than a passing resemblance to the long-haired movement of that time, years before the humans had taken their full-on path toward world destruction.

In fact, my parents had even dressed the part of hippies. My mom usually wore her hair in a long, graying braid, and she favored baggy jeans, or sometimes ankle-length dresses. My father, almost always in a beat-up leather hat and faded work clothes, had sported a heavy commune-style beard. And they kept a large collection of books, magazines, and other print-based relics from the era before 7-4 Day. I'd read most of the material myself.

Now I picked up a silicone circuit board and examined the chip array. It was from a top-of-the-line processor, as far as I could tell anyway.

"You were always a mad-professor type," I said.

"Well, in some ways you're right, Hays. In others, though . . . Well, that was actually a bit of a pose," he said. "A charade. A bold-faced lie, if you will."

He opened the door of a closet crammed with more junk. The closet's back wall swung inward, revealing a concrete staircase that led down under the earth. The steps were old and worn. The passageway must have been here all along, but I never knew that it existed. *Or that I had a sister, of course.*

I gave him a sharp glance. "Another thing that was too risky to tell me about?"

"Probably still is," he said, unperturbed. "Come this way. It's time you knew."

"It's a fallout shelter," my mother said, coming up behind us. "People built them in the old days so they could hide in case there was a nuclear war. That's part of why we moved to this place. It was a good space for our laboratory."

"*Laboratory?* You have a *laboratory?* What are you doing with a —"

She touched her finger to my lips to shush me. "Look first," she said. "Talk later."

The large underground chamber we had entered was very much the opposite of the chaos and goofy ineptitude featured upstairs. Everything in it was cutting-edge, modern, ordered, very precise.

There were gleaming metal worktables, well-organized racks of equipment, a row of incubating chambers. Vats filled with clear liquid appeared to have living tissue growing in them. Through a doorway, I glimpsed a fully equipped surgical operating room.

My *parents* had set up all this? A pair of gentle, aging homebodies? Two hippies?

My mother guided me into a side room that had a few comfortable chairs, a couch, and an ancient video apparatus known as a television— I'd never seen a real one, only pictures of them.

"We've saved these all this time, Hays, hoping you'd see them someday. And these discs you *should* watch," she said. "They're what used to be called 'home movies.' You're the star of most of them."

Chapter 40

I PUT IN a disc, and the TV screen came alive with grainy images that must have been shot with a camera as old as the television.

A cute little boy, about age three, was toddling along at his mother's side, clinging to her hand. They were walking toward a pebbly beach on a lake with a house in the background.

The smiling, familiar woman was short-haired, young, and very beautiful. One of the most beautiful women I'd ever seen, actually. She could have easily been a movie star.

The boy was moving along awkwardly, making happy infantile sounds as only a human baby would. Elite children of that age—raised in vitro for a full twenty-four months—were as physically coordinated as human ten-year-olds and already talking coherently. Elite children also didn't have belly buttons, and this one had an outie as big as a grown man's knuckle.

I kept watching with shocked fascination as the "home movie" images changed and continued to flicker gently before my eyes.

The same little boy lay peacefully asleep in bed, with his tiny hands curled beside his face. Very cute. Very tender as well.

Except, I realized suddenly, it wasn't a bed. *It was the table in an operating room.*

The beautiful woman stood nearby, but this time she wasn't smiling. She had her hands to her face, with tears flowing through her fingers. The clean-shaven father, looking serious and concerned, embraced her, patted her back repeatedly.

After a moment, she nodded against his shoulder. Then they both donned pale blue surgical gowns and masks.

The images on the screen shifted again to another scene. There was the boy, maybe a year older, running across the lawn — only now he was as swift and agile as a deer. The camera followed him as he raced through a forest obstacle course, making long swings from overhead handholds and leaping over walls.

It was the very same kind of athletic training I'd received—and excelled at—when I'd first entered Elite schools.

The next images were of the boy and his father sitting in the living room of the house, in front of a comfortable fire, playing four-dimensional chess. The boy was winning the game, and winning easily.

And then there was the same boy, age five now, swimming the butterfly stroke in the lake, really motoring. And now he was hauling himself out of the water onto the wooden planks of the dock as his father ran to him, holding a timepiece in his hand. The boy looked at the watch and began pumping his arm in the air as the father hugged him.

The camera zoomed in and the boy beamed—a smile I recognized only too well.

And now the camera panned back out, and the father reached down to pick up a towel so the boy could dry his preternaturally strong body—including his now navel-less torso.

Toys

The television screen went blank after that.

The tape was over.

I just kept sitting there, too stunned to move or even talk.

Those had been my parents. And I'd seen that boy before—in kindergarten pictures, in holiday and birthday stills... *it was me, of course.*

Portrait of a skunk as a young man.

Chapter 41

DURING THE NEXT hour or so, my mother and father tried to rationally, but gently, explain the incredible story behind the home movie I'd just watched.

I'll spare you, and myself, all of the painful details.

In a nutshell, they hadn't ever been biotech investors at all. They were famous scientists.

Human scientists.

They had been part of the core group of medical and genetic specialists who had pioneered the technology necessary to advance humans into superior Elites, thus hastening their progress with saving the world.

But after 7-4 Day—after whatever happened

during those mysterious twenty-four hours—my parents dropped out of the increasingly Elite-dominated society and went into hiding in the north country. Things were still chaotic in those first days, and their connections enabled them to retire to this faraway place, where their neighbors scarcely paid attention to them. They told the Elites they were retiring, but they'd begun to work in secret. And this time, they worked *against* the Elite nation and all that it stood for.

A centerpiece of the work was to turn me into a superenhanced human who could pass for an Elite—and who was, in many ways, more advanced than any Elite. They had essentially risked my life, and sanity, by sending me to live with the Elites as an undercover spy—without me having a clue about who or what I was.

"I'm sure you could use some time alone to think about all this," Mom said, tears leaking from her eyes. "Please don't think we came to the decision lightly, Hays. But we knew you'd make it. And we're so proud of you."

She gave me a quick kiss on the cheek, and she and Dad—also teary, but trying his best to hide it—left me alone.

But first, my father handed me another disc in a box that was labeled "7-4 Day."

I figured that something called "7-4 Day" couldn't be good news.

And it wasn't.

Wham! — no slow reveal, no fade-in. There were bodies everywhere. *Human* bodies. That was the film that completely blew whatever was left of my mind, and changed me forever.

I watched the terrifying pictures of the first attempt at eliminating all humans. As I did, tears flowed freely from my eyes, and they just wouldn't stop.

Chapter 42

AFTER I HAD viewed the 7-4 Day disc—three times—I just sat there for a couple of hours, numb all over, and changed. But then I didn't want to think about my past, my future, or anything else for a while. I walked back outside and started toward my car.

I was a human. The Elites were mass murderers—and now they wanted to finish the job once and for all.

They wanted humans to be extinct on the earth.

The back door of the house was open; Mom was in the kitchen, washing the dishes by hand. "I'm sorry," she said in a whisper as she saw me there.

"It's all right. I think I understand. I'm fine." I lied.

"By the way," she called to me as I passed, "Lucy's *sort of* your sister, but not genetically. And, obviously, you weren't raised together. So it's OK if you feel attracted to her. She's a beautiful girl, inside and out."

"*What are you saying?*" I raised my voice at my mother. Then I exploded. "I can't believe you said that! Even if you didn't care about your own family, don't you realize I have one of my own! I have Lizbeth. I have Chloe and April."

"Oh Hays, Hays, poor Hays. Don't pay any attention to *her*," said a second Mom, walking into the kitchen. This one was crying. "She's a mechanical clone—I had to make one. I just have too much to do around here. She's a great help, but she does say the most *stupid* things sometimes."

As if to drive home the point: "And I hate to break it to you," said the clone, "but it's true what they told you in the Elite hospital. Lizbeth isn't real eager to see you again. Of course, that tramp had already been sleeping with that bastard Moore—"

Mom put her hand over the clone's mouth and pushed her to the back of the kitchen, where she switched the chatty machine off.

"What was that all about?" I demanded to know. "Is it true?"

"Well, it can't have escaped your attention that Lizbeth is very ambitious," said my father, entering the kitchen from the living area.

"Right. And so was—I mean, so *am* I."

"Well, let's just say she isn't exactly intent on staying by your side," said Mom. "Oh Hays, I'm so sorry we're breaking all this to you. But it's important that you know the truth now. They are planning to exterminate all humans. Lizbeth is part of it. She knows a great deal about the final plan. Perhaps you could help us with her?"

I waved my hands for her to stop talking. I'd heard more than I could manage for right now. I needed to think, to have some space. So I walked away and hurried out to my car.

"Right now, I don't know who to believe," I called back to my parents.

Chapter 43

"WELCOME BACK, SIR," Elle Too said as I climbed into the driver's seat. I'd named her after my own car's attendant. "You seem unusually tense. Can I do anything to help you?"

I almost laughed. *Tense?* Try shell-shocked, or borderline suicidal. "The mood helmet, please," I said. "I'm fine, Elle, just fine. Thanks for asking."

I reclined the seat fully while her fingers slipped the padded helmet onto my head. I didn't have anything particular in mind, so I just surfed with the remote, trying out different ambiences.

I automatically skipped past high-adrenaline venues like sports, racing, and big-game hunting; I definitely needed something more soothing. After a couple of minutes, I came to a very popular selection titled "Behind Closed Doors—Shhhh!"

I didn't think this was what I needed—but maybe it was worth a look-see anyway. Couldn't hurt, right? The backdrop was a comfortable-looking room with old-fashioned furniture and a cheery fire crackling in the grate. A thick, soft rug was spread in front of it. A table was set with four glasses and a bottle of champagne in an ice bucket.

"Would you like company?" a voice said, but it was *inside* my head.

I hesitated. I needed some kind of escape—and maybe it was sensual pleasure that could help.

"Company could be nice," I said. "I'm definitely feeling a touch vulnerable."

"Select your guests: Female? Male? Animal? How many?"

"One female will do, thanks," I said.

Two of the champagne glasses disappeared.

"Select START indicator to begin ideation."

I moved my focus over the icon and willed the program to commence.

Bingo! I was inside the room, stretched out on the rug, feeling the fire's glow.

And that wasn't all I was feeling. A warm shape snuggled up against me. I could barely see the outlines, like disturbed air—but my senses told me it was definitely female.

I knew what I was supposed to do next. It was up to my imagination to fill her in. Whatever I wished for would come true.

I decided to let my subconscious take over and see what would happen. I closed my eyes and emptied my mind of everything but the touch of silken skin and a lemony fragrance that was intoxicating.

Lips brushed mine—soft, full, extremely kissable.

I enjoyed that for a lingering minute, letting the suspense build. I was relaxing; the images from the "home movies" were receding.

Then I took a peek to see who was in the room with me.

"What the?"

My eyes shot all the way open. The female figure lying beside me had shaggy blond hair, the most beautiful blue eyes, and a face that was a dead ringer for that of my sister, Lucy.

That was what was lurking deep in my imagination? Lucy? That criminal. A human? It had to be a fluke, I told myself. The idea was only there because of what my mother's clone had suggested in the kitchen.

But Lucy's mouth couldn't have tasted sweeter, and she definitely had a great body. And—she wanted me. God, I was vulnerable, wasn't I?

Then I thought—how could it hurt? She was literally a figment of my imagination. Just a fantasy, a dream girl, harmless adult entertainment.

"Tell me your name," I said, curious about what she would say.

She gave me a sly look—like she knew what I was thinking.

Suddenly, a loud *bang bang bang* sounded. It took me a few seconds to realize someone was knocking on the window of the car.

Chapter 44

I YANKED OFF the mood helmet and rolled down the pod's window. *Well, what do you know?*

The real Lucy was standing there, watching me with a frown, or maybe it was a self-satisfied smirk. Humans were known to be prudish, even puritanical, after all.

"You look like you were sucking on a lemon slice," she said. "Playdate?"

"For God's sake, can't anyone have some privacy around here?"

Her face turned serious. "Let's not hate each other for the moment. We got off to a bad start, I know, but we were just doing what we had to."

"I *had* to do what I did, yeah. But I don't get why you and your thugs *had* to attack me."

"Maybe we're thugs to Elites — but to humans, we're freedom fighters. Like I told you, we weren't out to kill you — we just needed to make it look that way. Our object was to bring you here…"

"Well, here I am. My life is a total wasteland now. Happy?"

She sighed. "Ecstatic. I'm on my way to go fishing. Want to come?"

Fishing? How crazy was that? But I did have a few questions for Lucy. So many questions, I didn't know where to start.

So I put away the mood helmet, climbed out of the car, and walked with her toward the beach.

"Don't take this as a compliment, but you know more about high-level Elite operations than any other human in the world," Lucy said. "That makes you extremely valuable to us. You've even been called 'the Savior'!"

I snorted with amusement. "I've just found out that everything I ever believed is a lie — and that my parents are the ones who started the lie. So now I should just take your side and join the human race in oblivion? I should help to *save* them?"

"I certainly understand your feelings, Hays,

James Patterson

but you'd better believe they're getting ready to wipe us out—soon. That's right, I said *us*."

Actually, I couldn't argue with what Lucy said. I'd heard it myself from President Jacklin.

"You're probably angry at your mother and father," Lucy continued. "But think about how hard it must have been for them. Performing surgery on their own little boy, then sending him away into the enemy's camp. Maybe to die."

Suddenly, I remembered the home movie scene of Mom weeping inside the operating room.

Then it struck me how Lucy had phrased that last sentence.

"*My* mother and father?" I said. "So it's true that you're not really my sister?"

"My own parents were their best friends. My folks died when I was a baby, and they adopted me. But you and I do have a biological connection. Your mom and dad enhanced me surgically, just like they did for you, beano. Our brains have implants from the same chip set, and some of our organ tissue is cloned from the same sources. You do the biology."

Shaking my head in confusion, I stepped into the boathouse, which was filled with familiar old smells of fishy water and musty equipment, and started loading gear into the skiff.

"That's terrible, losing parents so young," I said. "Both at once? Some kind of accident?"

"No, it was totally deliberate," she said. "The Elites declared them enemies of the state—and then executed them. Your friend Jax Moore did the job himself. Someday I'll cut off both his murdering hands, fry 'em in bacon grease, and eat them."

"Ah," I said, "well put."

Chapter 45

LUCY SAT PERCHED in the bow of the skiff as I rowed out onto the clear, smooth waters of the bay. Even though she'd had a lifetime to absorb it, the pain of her parents' death still must have cut very deep. It certainly seemed that way. I was starting to understand humans better, and to feel something for them—other than contempt, that is.

"Finally, some unexplained things are starting to fall into place," I said. "I couldn't figure out what my sensors were telling me that night. I was sure you weren't an Elite. But I didn't know anything about humans being able to be enhanced to this degree."

She nodded. "Just to set the record straight—

I'm *more* enhanced than you are. I came along later and the technology was improved. Sorry, *bro*."

I stopped rowing in mid-stroke. "You've got to be joking. You *are*, aren't you?"

"I'm simply stating a scientific fact."

"Not possible," I said, and dropped the oars back into the water.

"You think I *can't* compete with you?"

I didn't bother to answer.

"Remember, I've seen you in action. But you've never really seen *my* moves," she continued to taunt in a lighthearted way.

I shrugged. "I don't need to see your moves. I know what I'm capable of. Few, if any, *Elites* can match me for strength, speed, problem solving."

Lucy put her fists on her hips. "You're starting to make me very mad. I'll race you to the house."

"From here?" I glanced around. We were about a mile from the beach.

"Why not? You can swim, can't you, *superman*?"

I shook my head and grinned. "I'll do my best. What are the stakes?"

"Sheer satisfaction, and bragging rights, of course."

She kicked off her sneakers, unbuttoned her shirt and tossed it aside. Then she wriggled out of her jeans, leaving herself in a halter top and panties—which were turquoise blue and nicely revealing.

I pulled off my boots and shirt and stood up.

"You're going to leave your pants on?" she said.

The uncomfortable truth was that when I'd been hurrying to buy new clothes, I'd forgotten to get underwear.

"I'll take my chances."

"Whatever you say, hotshot. Quit staring at my legs though."

"Sorry. But, you know, there they are."

"Not for long. Ready?"

"Any time."

"How about *now!*"

We dove off the boat at the same instant, both with powerful arcing leaps that carried us a good ten yards.

But actually, Lucy hit the water at least a couple of feet ahead of me. I couldn't believe it.

I stayed under for another hundred yards, aware of Lucy right beside me. She was slicing through the water like a seal.

By the time we broke the surface, her lead had increased to half a body length, and those strong thighs of hers were churning along—next to my head.

I attacked the remaining distance with ferocious strokes, moving faster than the fastest human could run.

But by the time my toes found the sandy bottom, she was scampering up the beach, her turquoise behind twitching back and forth as if it were waving good-bye.

That iced it.

I was damned if I was going to let her outrun me too.

With the two of us bounding along like giant, insane grasshoppers, I poured on everything I had, springing after her in huge stretching leaps, barely skimming the ground when I touched down. Each time, my longer legs gained a step on her, and as the house came into sight and loomed closer, the two of us were in a dead heat.

I couldn't let her win—not *twice* in the same race.

I landed on the porch an instant before Lucy

did. But before I could declare any kind of victory, she turned and said, "I let you win—*the run*."

Then my "sister" disappeared inside the house.

Chapter 46

I HAD TO retrieve the skiff, and when I got back to the house, my father was sitting out on the porch. Just the sight of Dad there brought back the most powerful memories of past times at the lake.

"I'd like to chat," I told him. "I really need to talk some things through. Like 7-4 Day."

"Can't help you," he said, shaking his head. "I'm a clone."

Like Mom's, this one appeared to be an exact duplicate—with a beard, hat, and worn-out work clothes. Anticipating my next question, it said, "We take care of most of the chores and require no pay. Slavery at its very best."

"Where's my father then?"

"Working in the lab. Where else? Nice chatting with you, *son*."

Shaking my head, but smiling at the "slavery" line, I walked down the stairway to the underground lab and found my father sitting in front of a bank of monitors that lined one wall.

Some of them showed maps of different areas around the globe and contained colored clusters that looked like they represented populations. Others were flashing coded messages.

"Feeling better?" Dad asked, swinging his chair around to face me.

"Suppose I did agree to fight against the Elites," I said. "Then what happens?"

He pointed to the bank of monitors. "I'm in contact with resistance leaders around the world. We were just discussing you."

"Around the world? What are you talking about now? There's nothing out there but... savages."

"That's what the Elite leadership wants everybody to believe, Hays. Things are actually much more organized on our side than they like to let on."

So, more government lies. Supposedly, Elites

made up only about 5 percent of the world's population. But they controlled North America, and their military power kept the rest of the world cowed into submission. The official story was that other continents were crowded with humans, dirty and barbaric, and the only Elites actually allowed to travel there were government and corporate insiders.

So what was the *real* story? I suspected that I was about to find out.

Chapter 47

I SPENT THE remainder of that evening in the lab with my father, learning the basics of the communications code and the other systems that the human resistance used. The real truth was that I just wanted to spend time with him, possibly get to know him better. Obviously, I hadn't known before who he was.

After several hours, Dad stretched and pushed his work chair back wearily.

"I'm going to get a little rest, Hays," he said. "I'm getting to be an old fart, and after all, *I'm only human.*" He smiled at his little joke. But so did I.

"I'll stay here. I'm not all that sleepy." In fact, I was antsy—I wanted to *do* something to help the humans, especially my mom and dad.

Toys

As he was leaving, my father said, "There's something else you should think about. Toys might seem like harmless fun to you, as they do to most people, but they can be sinister and very dangerous. I'm not exaggerating for effect. These toys are not what they seem."

"How's that? They're just harmless entertainment."

"No, they're not. The Elites have been pushing them out into society because they want them to be like a drug—or a cult religion. The very best toys take you away from the real world so you don't have to deal with it. Elites *do* have some human qualities, including a modicum of compassion. Most of them would be a lot more concerned about what happens to us if they didn't spend so much time in toyland. But the leaders want it that way. It's part of their plan to keep total control. Even over other Elites."

He leaned over and kissed the top of my head, the way he'd done at bedtime when I was a little boy. It was very touching, and I fought with myself not to get sentimental and gooey.

"I love you, son," he said simply.

I didn't say anything back to him. I just

couldn't. I guess I was still too close to my Elite life.

I watched him trudge away, and it reminded me of what a heavy burden he and my mother had carried all these years—the endless, thankless work they'd done while living in secrecy and in fear of being caught, knowing that it was only a matter of time before the Elites moved to exterminate "the human menace."

Which now included me.

At heart though, I couldn't help believing that there was nothing I could do to make a difference—human resistance was futile. The Elite population might still be relatively small, but their military and weaponry were so sophisticated that they could eliminate most of the world's humans in a succession of swift strikes. Then they'd swarm over the globe with their cruel efficiency, finishing off the survivors.

At least the quandary gave me something to think about—other than the ruin of the perfect life I'd taken for granted and never really understood worth a damn.

I was still sitting in the lab an hour later when

my acute hearing picked up sounds outside that didn't belong.

I held my breath, concentrating, trying to figure the noises out.

Someone was approaching—some*ones*. I counted forty-seven of them—moving stealthily from the bay toward the house, and now fanning out to surround it.

I jumped out of my chair and sprinted for the stairs—just as an alarm siren started blaring throughout the house.

"It's Elites—they're attacking!" I shouted. "They're everywhere!"

Chapter 48

I RUSHED UPSTAIRS and saw that my mother and father, still in their nightclothes, had already taken up defensive positions at the windows on the main floor. The clones were there too. They all had laser rifles, and Dad tossed me one as I ran into the living room.

"We'll hold them off from here, Hays. You get outside. Try to get behind them," he said. "No mercy. They won't show any to us."

"I know," I said. "They hate us skunks." *I know exactly what they're thinking. Because I used to think that way myself.*

My father looked fierce, magnificent, like an old warrior who relished a battle against impossible odds. My mother, too, was calm and fearless; she'd never been more beautiful or impressive than she was right then.

"Where's Lucy?" I asked them.

My mother just shook her head. "She's probably escaped already, Hays. Lucy can't be captured here. She's too important."

I hugged them both quickly, then raced out the back of the house and across the lawn. On the way, my enhanced night vision picked out a dozen of the approaching black-clad figures.

Killers—assassins! They mean to exterminate my family. And me.

These were highly trained Elite soldiers, and they spotted me too. Blasts of weapon fire lit my path as I ran for the cover of trees.

Weaving side to side, keeping low to the ground, I barely made it to the shelter of the woods. The terrain there was imprinted in my childhood memory. I knew every tree to hide behind as I prepared my ambush. But there were so many of them, against so few of us. Lucy would have helped—but she was too important to be captured.

Three commandos had spotted me and were now moving quickly in my direction. Their mistake—or arrogance. A single horizontal sweep with my rifle cut the trio into lumps of smoking flesh.

I sprinted past the ruined bodies, dodging from tree to tree, picking off a few more Elite soldiers as they appeared. I sensed rapid movement behind me. I barely had time to drop to a crouch as a laser streak flashed past my face, so close it singed my cheek.

I dropped my rifle and leaped up sideways into a tree crotch. The shooter spun frantically back and forth, trying to spot me again. I dove at him with both hands outstretched. His spine popped as I wrenched his head clear around. It was quite possibly the worst sound I'd ever heard.

I told myself I had no choice. *These Elites are here to slaughter us. I have no allegiance to them. It's kill—or be killed.*

Chapter 49

I HELPED MYSELF to the dead man's weapon and ran straight toward the main cadre of attackers, who were blitzing my parents' house with relentless fire. Hard to comprehend—the place where you grew up under a murderous attack like this.

They were swarming inside, overrunning the place, as I came up behind them. Unfortunately, I didn't see my mother or father anywhere. Or Lucy either. The fighting was hand to hand now. Finally, I caught a glimpse of Mom swinging an old cast-iron skillet, braining one of them. She was fighting side by side with her faithful clone.

Then the unthinkable happened. A tremendous fireball erupted into the sky. It fell and struck the roof of our house. Next came an explosion of flaming timbers and furnishings, the flailing limbs of Elite soldiers, their horrifying cries.

Their comrades had fired a rocket into the heart of the battle, sacrificing their own without a second thought. That was how Elites fought.

I stared in horror and disbelief as the burning debris rained down around me.

"Mom! Dad!" I yelled. "Where are you?"

It didn't take me long to find them—two charred corpses, their hands extending toward each other as if they'd been reaching out to touch one last time.

How could anyone kill these good people? Massacre them? Who would do such a cowardly thing? But I knew the answer to that: Elites had already annihilated hundreds of millions of humans. What were a few more?

Standing there with my heart breaking, I whispered, "I love you, Dad. I love you, Mom." I hated myself for not saying it more when they were alive. "You will have your revenge. I promise that—at least that."

My God, I had just seen both my parents—

dead. I couldn't make myself think straight, could barely capture a breath.

Numb with shock—ready to die now myself—I swung around to fight the rest of the Elites. I could see them creeping out of the woods.

Suddenly, I hated them, hated all Elites—but especially their leader, whoever had planned this cowardly attack.

Then I saw who it was. On the crest of a nearby hill, Jax Moore was walking toward what remained of our house. He was dressed as a commando, gun in hand, smoking one of his victory cigars.

I had lost my concentration. A flying body slammed into me and threw me to the ground, gripping me in an iron-tight headlock. I hadn't seen him coming.

"Don't fight me!" Lucy whispered into my ear.

Chapter 50

"JAX MOORE!" I told her. "He's behind this."

"Doesn't matter. Not now. This isn't the time or place, Hays. *Come with me!*" Lucy took off then — fast. "Hays, *come!*"

"Where have you been?" I called, racing behind Lucy as she headed toward the bay. Maybe she *could* run faster than me? Or was it because my legs felt like nothing right now? I could hardly breathe, and I couldn't get the image of my murdered parents out of my mind. The tragedy, the outrage. And Jax Moore, that bastard!

"Killing the commandos — where do you think I've been? I just couldn't kill enough. I finished off that rocket crew — they were about to fire again and take you out. I'm sorry we couldn't save your mother and father. Or stop to kill that fucker Moore!"

Yes, so was I — and on top of everything else, now I owed Lucy my life!

She must have had some kind of signaling device because, as we got close to the water, the gleaming black shape of a car came rising up out of a well-hidden underground chamber. It was the same style as my own car back in New Lake City — a no-nonsense model built for speed and maneuverability.

"Let me drive," I said. I needed to drive *very fast*. I needed to stop seeing the faces of my parents — murdered.

"You're in no shape, Hays. You're riding in the trunk."

"What?"

"If we meet anybody, I smile and wave. I'm just a silly, harmless woman out for a ride. But *you* look like you've been eating babies for dinner — they'd freak out. Besides, you're all worked up, and you might do something stupid."

"I don't do stupid things," I said, although a recent list to the contrary popped into my mind.

"Shut *up* and get in, Hays. They're gaining on us. We have seconds to get out of here. Seriously, Hays. Come, or stay here and die."

Chapter 51

I CURSED OUT loud, but then I jumped into the open trunk as Lucy slammed down the lid.

A moment later, the car shot forward, skimmed the surface of the water for a minute, then landed under expert control on the opposite shore.

Lucy's voice came through the alloy barrier: "Don't worry your pretty little head. I know these back roads cold, and I know exactly where we're going."

"Where's that?" I called back from the trunk. "Don't leave me — *in the dark.*"

"Canada."

"No way!" The Canadian border was at least four hundred miles away. I struggled angrily to sit upright, but succeeded only in banging my head. "You expect me to stay in here for an hour and a half?" I yelled.

"Longer than that, I'm afraid. Sorry. We've got to get across the border station, then on into New Vancouver. There'll be cars all around us. And police."

"I can break out of the trunk in a second," I warned. "You have no idea."

"Go ahead—that'll get us killed for sure. See what I mean about doing something stupid?"

I slumped back down again. She was right, of course. We drove the next couple of minutes in silence. I had to admit, she was an expert behind the wheel. I could tell from the way the car cornered— we were moving at close to top ground speed.

"I loved your parents too, you know." Lucy finally spoke again. "Sorry if I seem cold, but we don't have time to grieve right now."

That reminded me that her own parents had also been killed by Elites. By that monster Jax Moore. My old boss. Lizbeth's boss too. And what else was he to my wife?

I exhaled sadly. "How did we get into this awful mess? The big picture?"

"Humans made the mess, to start with," Lucy said. "Elites got that eco-disaster stopped, but now they're making a worse one. It will give them what they think they want, a sterile, orderly world. But it will leave their kind with a huge weakness — they don't have much in the way of imagination. Something about all that helpful machinery in their brains. It makes them almost too rational to take the necessary creative risks. You probably didn't know this, but Elites don't even design the machines. They have covert facilities where they force human scientists to do it."

I'd never even heard a whisper about that — it must have been one of the most closely guarded state secrets. But I didn't say anything. In the insane new picture of the world I was forming, it made perfect sense.

"That's the one thought in all this that gives me a glimmer of satisfaction," Lucy said. "Without humans, the Elites are probably going to end up dying of boredom. The irony of it is almost poetic."

I settled deeper into the trunk, which wasn't actually all that uncomfortable. It was the recent memories in my head that were torture—images of my murdered mother and father, repeating themselves over and over. Images of Lizbeth and our daughters. Would I ever see them again? Finally, an image of Jax Moore smoking that victory cigar of his.

"I don't suppose you can think of anything cheerful to talk about," I said. I sure couldn't.

"Well—do you remember, when you were five, playing a game with a little girl?" Her voice was softer now.

I frowned—it seemed an odd question. But I tried to think back.

"What kind of game?" I asked. "Give me a little more to go on."

"It was on the beach at your parents' house. She'd find small stones in the sand and bring them to you, and you'd build them up into a castle. The two of you would do it over and over, building a new castle every day. Never tiring of the game."

A flicker of memory crossed my mind. A towheaded, blue-eyed toddler hurrying toward me with a few stones clutched in her tiny fists, watching with solemn fascination as I fitted them together into a crude wall or tower, oftentimes directing the castle's construction, then tottering off to fetch another handful.

"That was you?" I asked. "That pretty little blond girl?"

"That was me, Hays. And you. I had such a crush on you. When you were five."

Chapter 52

UNFORTUNATELY, THE ACTION and drama wasn't stopping. How could it with President Jacklin's plan against the humans under way? An hour later, Lucy jumped out of the car and hurried toward two grizzled pilots who were about to climb into a jet parked on the tarmac. The locale was a small private airport just outside New Vancouver that operated luxury aircraft for Elite corporate executives and military officers with special clearance to travel into Human Wasteland.

I was still crowded in the car trunk, watching through a slightly open lid.

"Hey, could you guys give a girl a lift?" she called to them as she approached.

They stopped and turned, looking amused at what they saw. While they stared at Lucy, I eased out of the trunk and moved around behind them.

"Where you going, sweetheart?" the older of the two said.

Lucy had both hands on her hips, and the top buttons of her blouse were undone. Nothing too understated about that; nothing too understated about Lucy, period.

"I'm not real particular. Anywhere but here. You follow me, Captain?"

"We're not supposed to carry unauthorized passengers," the younger one said. He had a close, army-style haircut, looked buff, and was definitely checking her out.

"People do a lot of things they're not supposed to," Lucy answered back. "Or so they tell me."

The older one laughed out loud. "Got yourself in a little trouble?"

"Let's just say I need to relocate — quickly — and I'm flat broke. That give you the picture?"

"Well, it's pretty tight up in the cockpit, but we could probably sneak you in."

"I'll be fine. I can be *very* flexible."

"I'm not sure about this," the younger pilot said nervously. "We could get in trouble, Mel. Couldn't we?"

"Come on, who's going to know?" his partner said with a cocky shrug. "Nobody cares who flies *out* of the country."

"You want a peek at the cargo first?" Lucy said. She smiled cheerfully and reached to unbutton her blouse another notch or two.

Well, that eliminated resistance for both of them. As they stepped closer to her, I came up behind, grabbed a handful of hair from each, and bashed their heads together. Just hard enough to knock the pilots out.

"Nice work, Hays," Lucy said and grinned. "But I'm *still* driving."

I was done arguing with her—at least for right now. She was the one, after all, who was *too important to be captured*. I wondered what that was all about.

"I'll let the passengers know there's been a change in flight plans," I said.

"Try to be subtle, Hays."

"Definitely."

We jumped on board, with Lucy ducking into the cockpit and me heading back into the passenger compartment.

Chapter 53

SUBTLE, I REMINDED myself. *That is certainly sound advice under the circumstances. We are, after all, hijacking this plane.*

Unfortunately, when I walked into the cabin, which was decked out like a luxury hotel suite—with plush couches, a full bar, and the latest entertainment devices from the Toyz Corporation—the three executive types seated there weren't particularly overjoyed to see me on board.

I guess I could understand why. They were just getting acquainted with the other passengers: two beautiful and well-endowed female androids who were at the preflight teasing stage of their "coffee, tea, or me" routine. And the "me" part could be taken quite literally.

"What are *you* doing in here?" the oldest of the businessmen asked, probably the boss. "We didn't order any male androids."

The executive brushed a partially undressed female companion off his lap and stood, glaring at me with the self-assured look of somebody used to being in charge.

Subtle, Hays.

I snapped to attention and gave him a salute. "I'm with the Agency of Change," I answered. "I'm on a mission here."

I *was* on a mission—to find something in the compartment I could use as a weapon. These three execs might not be trained fighters, but they weren't ordinary humans, either—they were Elite males, and I didn't have the edge of surprise I'd had with the pilots. "We're bringing a bomb simulator on board. It's a prototype...for wiping out human cities. Don't worry, there's no danger to any of you. This is President Jacklin's initiative."

The hostility on their faces changed to interest, and duty. So now what did I tell them?

"The machine will be loaded on in just a minute," I said as I sidestepped into a storage area that held metal canisters of fire retardant. I wrenched one of them from its rack. It would have to do.

The plane had suddenly started forward in a smooth glide that, at first, was barely perceptible. The senior executive who'd first challenged me did it again. "The door's still open! And if the prototype's coming in, why are we moving?" he asked.

"To give you a running start," I said and spun around with the heavy canister, lashing it at his jaw. It connected with a *rinnng* that vibrated through my fingers all the way to my teeth.

As he staggered away, I planted my boot in his chest and shoved him, flailing and yelping, out the open door to the tarmac below. Before I could recover my balance, the other two gents piled onto me. I could tell by the way they moved that they had military backgrounds.

I was still clutching the canister in my hands, so I snapped the seal off the nozzle. I aimed it at them. Then I coated the men with a blast of gooey, greenish fire retardant.

"What the hell!" one of them yelled. "I can't see!"

They reeled away, crashing into each other, blinded for the moment. Next, I used the canister to bludgeon them out the door behind their bossy friend.

Then I turned my attention to the two androids. "Ladies, I'm afraid you get off here too!" They were only too happy to oblige.

"That's your idea of *subtle*?" I heard Lucy call from up front. "Now shut the damn door!"

Chapter 54

IT TOOK SOME wrestling to get the plane's door closed. Seconds later though, we were off, streaking out across the vast expanse of the North Pacific—toward only Lucy knew precisely where, and why.

After a few hours of resting back in the cabin, I finally went up in the cockpit with her. "Now what happens?" I asked.

"More trouble, I'm afraid. The radar shows an interceptor craft, and it's gaining on us. We've got maybe ten minutes before it catches up. They *really* don't want you to get away, Hays."

"Maybe Lizbeth just wants me back."

"No offense, but I doubt that very much. You are a human, Hays. She's *High* Elite, and I don't mean that as a compliment. The two of you are oil and water."

She gazed at me calmly, but we both had an idea of what was coming next. The interceptor was a smart-missile that would clamp onto our plane, cut a hole through the fuselage, and unleash a team of highly trained Elite commandos inside.

"We're going to have to bail out," she said. "You've used a Deathwish Suit before, haven't you?"

"Unfortunately, yes," I answered. "Deathwish Suit" was a pejorative nickname for superinsulated silicone uniforms with jet-propulsion packs and parachutes. They were designed for high-altitude bailouts, like this one would be. The jetpacks would last an hour, keeping you aloft, then you needed to pop the chute and hope for a pinpoint landing.

"Come in here and put one on," she said. "I'm trying to contact friends in Russia who might help us. But it's going to be down to the wire."

"Just the way I like it," I said.

"You're such a liar."

"Not me. *Everybody else.*"

Chapter 55

THE ATTACK CAME much faster than Lucy or I would have liked. With a harsh grinding sound, the interceptor latched like a giant, metal remora onto the outside of the jet. It rocked us sideways, but the Elites apparently didn't want to knock us out of control and risk a crash. Maybe I was still usable to them—or to Lizbeth. Or maybe Jax Moore wanted to kill me himself.

I was snuggled up beside the rear cargo-hatch controls, my body wedged tightly into a storage space, my feet braced against a wall.

A laser saw from the interceptor, with a sharp hiss, had already started to cut into metal. A smoldering line appeared in our hull as the beam sliced through.

In less than a minute, the cutout fell inward, and two well-built Elite guards charged through, with three more right behind them. They were armed with assault rifles and wearing their own Deathwish Suits, ready for anything.

Well, not anything.

I dropped the cargo hatch!

Instantly, a ferocious wind sprang up inside the plane.

The first two commandos were too shocked and surprised to grab hold of anything. The suction pulled them flying through the cabin, then shot them out the hatch into the dark ether.

The same could be said for just about everything else that wasn't fastened down tightly. Bottles from the bar flew past me like a hail of bullets, along with luggage, wads of plush upholstery, entire cabinets that had been torn from the walls.

Then my luck turned bad again. *Our* luck, since Lucy was involved now too. The cutout section of hull was wrenched off the floor and came spinning along with the rest of the debris — but it hit the hatch opening flat, blocking most of it.

When the three remaining commandos got sucked toward the hatch, they slammed into the hull cutout instead. Not good for me. Suddenly, it was three against one, and these guys were trained to maim, then kill.

Of course, I tried to remind myself, *so am I.*

I unwedged myself, pointed my feet at them, and let go of my grip. The wind shot me toward the hatch like a human pile driver. *This certainly should be interesting. If I survive.*

Chapter 56

PROVING THAT I still had "it," I slammed into two of the muscular commandos, a boot planted squarely in each man's chest. The force of our impact caved in the hull section, folding it in the middle. It blew out through the hatch and *we went with it,* twisting into the air outside with gut-wrenching speed.

I grabbed hold of the nearest commando's throat, then gave my jetpack a hard blast.

The two of us broke free from the others and rocketed away, punching and kneeing each other viciously as we struggled for control of his rifle.

His buddies were quick to follow, moving faster than I could with my unwilling passenger in tow. Flashing bursts of laser fire started hissing past us.

I managed to spin the commando around and into a headlock with the rifle pinned across his throat. As best I could, I was using him as a shield.

His "buddies" didn't hesitate for a second. They continued to fire mercilessly. The tough skin of the Deathwish Suits kept the blasts from traveling all the way through, but I suffered the shock of successive shots hitting his body. I felt him convulse—then go limp in my arms.

Hanging on to the rifle, I curled myself up tightly and shoved the dead body into their path. Then I jetted away in a series of sharp, erratic somersaults. That bought me a few seconds, long enough to turn around and start shooting back.

That was when another Deathwish-Suited figure came spinning into sight.

Lucy in the sky—no diamonds!

She was zooming in behind the pair of commandos, so they didn't see her—not until she crashed piggyback onto one Elite's shoulders. She locked the poor guy's neck between her thighs in a scissor hold. Then her hands snapped his neck, tearing off his helmet with such fury that I was surprised when his head wasn't still inside it.

As she rode that flopping body past the other commando, the sight distracted him for the instant I needed to fire off several shots. The lasers slammed his back; his hands jerked up and tossed his rifle into the icy wind rushing around us.

Lucy released her grip on the dead man she was straddling, and he sailed away, out to join his brethren in a long, final plunge to oblivion in the wild waters of the Bering Sea.

Lucy turned, grinned rather insanely, and gave me a double thumbs-up.

For my part, I grinned insanely back at her, wondering what I'd gotten myself into with this crazy, but obviously brave and impressive, human woman.

Book Three

THE EUROPEAN TOUR

Chapter 57

THE INSANE GRINS and double thumbs-ups between Lucy and me were long gone and almost forgotten now. Unfortunately, and as promised, flying in a Deathwish Suit was no joyride. I had to fight my way through the fierce air currents that tossed me around like a snowflake, and my body took a relentless, terrible pounding.

But the more serious problem was that our jetpack charges were running low. Lucy and I conserved some fuel by dropping into nearly heart-stopping free falls—then gave the jets a blast to lunge our bodies forward again.

But by the time we sighted land, still far away, we were running on empty.

I saw Lucy straighten her body like a high

diver leaping off a cliff, cut in her jets for a final burst of juice, and shoot forward in a long, arcing glide.

Now what? Follow the kamikaze, of course.

I did the same as Lucy, staying a few yards behind her. *Wherever* we hit, it was going to be together. Matching grave sites? That seemed a likely possibility.

Gravity sucked us downward with dizzying speed, hurling us straight toward frothing coastal breakers. At the last possible second, Lucy popped her parachute. So did I.

My chute engaged with a jolt that yanked me full around, but I still plunged the last couple hundred feet with the speed of a supercharged Mercedes on an open highway. I hit the shoreline in a tumbling roll that sent a white-hot shock through my blood and bones.

Then I bounced and skittered for a good ten to fifteen seconds before I finally skidded to a stop, face to face with an unresponsive boulder.

At least the *earth* was solid underneath me. I'd had more than enough *sky*.

Lucy was about fifty yards away, just getting to her feet.

I walked to join her, taking in the surroundings. Wherever we were, this place was damned *cold*; it might have been summer back in New Lake City, but here, the ground was half-frozen tundra. It stretched unbroken to the horizon, fading into the misted-over gray light of early morning.

All of a sudden I spotted a small blur moving in the distance—which quickly turned out to be a *scene from an earlier century*.

Unbelievable!

Two dozen fierce-looking men mounted on shaggy horses and wearing animal skins were riding toward us with astonishing speed. They were black-haired and golden-skinned, not very tall but powerfully built. They sat on their ponies with a confidence and ease that suggested they'd grown up on them.

I got the feeling that the grins on their faces would stay there even if their heads were being cut off—and probably *had* stayed on while they were cutting off other people's heads.

As they got close, the wings of their V-formation pulled ahead to form a circle, completely surrounding Lucy and me.

They'd done this before, hadn't they?

"Oh no," I said quietly.

The leader leaped off his still-moving horse, landing as nimbly and as well balanced as a cat would, and strode toward us, rifle in hand.

He completely ignored me, throwing open his arms and bellowing a word that sounded like *"Mehkween!"*

"Tazh Khan!" Lucy cried back, and then she hurried past me into his waiting embrace. The two of them hugged like long-lost lovers, then they talked excitedly and very rapidly in a language that was like nothing I'd ever heard or read.

Hoo boy! So these were the "friends" she'd contacted to help us save the human race from extinction?

Things didn't look too good for us skunks.

Chapter 58

"THERE ARE MANY tribes—and nations—out here in the real world," Lucy explained to me a few minutes later. We were riding horses—side by side. In Russia. Siberia, I believe.

"Is he a former boyfriend?" I asked.

"Certainly preferable to your wife," she answered. "But no, Tazh Khan is just a good friend. We've fought the Elites together and kicked some butt."

"Why do they call you *Mehkween*?" I asked next, half shouting over the swirling wind that was blowing down like a twister from the frozen north.

"It's Megwin," she answered. "That's what my parents originally named me, and that's how

223

some resistance people know me. Lucy's just for the straight world. *You* can call me Lucy."

"Thanks much, Mehkween."

I let it go at that; it wasn't really much of a surprise compared to everything else that had happened. It turned out that Lucy/Megwin had worked with Tazh Khan and his men for years. Despite their savage appearance, they had not only modern weapons but modern communications technology—and this *was* the rendezvous she'd arranged for while we were in the plane.

Now the Mongols were taking us to a place where we'd get safe transport across Russia—to England, which, according to Lucy, remained quite civilized. As did France, Germany, Italy, Scandinavia.

There was another reason besides the strong winds that made talking difficult. Jouncing along on the ponies that they'd provided had my teeth hopelessly clacking together. Horseback riding had not been included in Agent of Change training; I'd never even been near a horse before.

I found out fast that it wasn't nearly as easy as these Mongol warriors made it look. Sitting astride the bony little beast was like getting kicked squarely in the ass with every single step. It didn't help that I was close to a foot taller than everybody except Lucy.

It didn't help, either, that while the Mongols adored Lucy/Megwin, they didn't seem to like me one bit—especially Tazh Khan. They didn't try to hide their mockery of my clumsy horsemanship. Perhaps to drive the point home, one of them would occasionally gallop away from the group to chase one of the large hares that popped up out of the ground and dashed away. In a blur of erratic, side-blitzing speed, the pony would hunt it down while the rider leaned out parallel to the ground with his bow and arrow and skewered it.

Hitting a target like that was roughly like shooting a snowflake in a blizzard. But they never seemed to miss.

"Ey!" Tazh Khan said, trotting up beside me. He might have been thirty years old, or sixty, and looked like he was made completely of leather and bone, like he had existed forever.

"Ey!" he repeated and rubbed his belly, then jerked his thumb toward his mouth—apparently asking if I was hungry.

I waited warily. I *was* hungry, but I had a hard enough time with ordinary human food and seriously doubted that whatever this barbarian horde ate was any improvement on, say, the human frankfurter.

A long knife suddenly appeared in his hand, its edge worn thin, almost to invisibility, by what had to have been thousands of honings.

He leaned forward to whisper in his mount's ear, gave it a couple of soothing pats, then touched the blade to one of the pulsing veins that ran along its neck. Hell — *he'd just cut his own horse!*

As blood welled out, Tazh Khan clasped his mouth over the open cut and sucked in a long, leisurely drink.

The pony never even flinched. Its vein was crisscrossed with neat scars, I now saw. These horses weren't just transportation, they were movable snack bars.

When he finished, he smeared some kind of ointment around the nicked flap of the animal's skin and closed the wound. *Quite the humanitarian,* I was thinking.

Then he surprised me with an offer of his knife.

I did nothing but shake my head.

Tazh Khan spat contemptuously. Then he reined away from me and gave his knife to Lucy.

She flashed me a grin that was as fierce as the men's — then, without hesitation, she helped herself to a quaff of blood from the neck of her own mount.

What a girl.

Chapter 59

A RIPPLE OF cruel laughter broke from the riders, along with a chain of jeering comments, obviously at my expense. It grated worse than the jolting I was receiving from the pony. My patience was wearing as thin as the razor-sharp edge of Tazh Khan's knife.

"What are they saying?" I asked Lucy, who now rode beside me, possibly to keep an eye on me. "Translate for me, please."

"Let's just say—in the kindest way—that you remind them of the scared rabbits they hunt." She seemed somewhat sympathetic, but mostly amused herself. *That* set me off even more.

"All right," I said. "Then I'm the rabbit. Keep your eye on this rabbit!"

I swung my leg over the pony's back and slid down to the ground. What a relief it was to have solid earth under my feet again.

Lucy's face turned puzzled, as well as concerned. "What are you doing, Hays? Don't get yourself trampled now."

"Tell them to *hunt* me," I said. "All of them at once. For real. No holding back. Catch me if they can!"

Her eyes widened and actually showed some fear. "Hays, no. They don't mean it personally—it's a cultural thing."

But I cut her short with an upraised palm. "Cultural thing, my ass—it's a *guy* thing. They're questioning my...you know..."

Reluctantly, she spoke a few rushed sentences to the nomadic band, now watching me curiously. When she finished, their laughter chorused again, this time even louder and harsher. Tazh Khan answered her back in his piggish language.

"He says you must be smarter than he thought," Lucy translated, "to take refuge in the knowledge that their tribal law forbids them from killing a crazy man."

I smiled tightly. "Tell him that if any of them

can hit me, then I *won't* take away their cute little bows and arrows and break them over my knee."

Lucy raised her eyes heavenward, but she swung back around to them and delivered the challenge.

That really pissed them off.

As their laughter turned to brutish scowls, I bounced around in a few goofy bunny hops, waggling my fingers above my head like ears.

Then I took off—moving extremely fast in long leaps but staying low to the ground.

In the blink of an eye, I had a thundering herd of agile horses and murder-bent wild men hot on my little, cotton bunny tail.

The first several riders came in swiftly and close to the ground, and so did their arrows, registering on my vision as dark particles that instantaneously grew in length as they approached.

I danced about a foot or so above them, letting them whir past under my feet.

The Mongol horsemen slowed to a trot and dropped their bows in utter amazement—but also chagrin.

Bunny Rabbit, one; Mongolians, zip.

The rest of the band tried a different tack,

galloping around me in a half circle and firing their arrows all at once in a pattern—a grid several feet high and wide, with the shots spaced carefully inside it. If their plan worked, I would look like a frog that crash-landed into a thornbush.

This time I leaped straight up into a somersault, twisting upside down and plucking a few of the arrows out of the air as they shot underneath me. Coming down, I hurled them back, whistling the darts right past the horsemen's ears.

With exclamations of despair, they tossed their bows onto the refuse pile already started by their comrades. I'd nearly won them all over.

Now only one rider was left facing me: Tazh Khan himself.

For a few long seconds, we locked gazes. Then, without haste, he nocked an arrow, took careful aim, and unleashed it straight at my throat.

I shifted aside just enough to take it in the hollow of my left shoulder. It punched clear through, protruding out my back.

It also hurt like a sonofabitch. Lord, it stung.

I sagged to my knees as Lucy came running up and put her arm around me. "Oh, Hays, you *fool*. You complete idiot."

"I'm fine—just like at the lake, I let them win."

"Tazh Khan's right—you're crazy," she then whispered angrily.

"Tell them they won," I said. "And if they'll get this damn arrow out of me, they can drink as much of my blood as they want."

Chapter 60

WELL, IT WAS a small price to pay—I heal quickly—but my Hays the Rabbit act won the horse soldiers over, even Tazh Khan, it seemed.

Toward evening, our merry band of Mongolians arrived at a small city, if you could call it that—a couple of square miles of gray streets and squat industrial buildings that rose up starkly out of the tundra. It was named Vlosk; mainly, it was a transport depot to ship ore from nearby mines, probably to Moscow and St. Petersburg.

Lucy had already arranged passage for us on one of the cargo rockets that made constant flights to North Sea ports.

Then we'd be taken straightaway to England,

where the human leaders we needed to meet were based—though Lucy told me there were also leadership councils in Berlin, Madrid, Stockholm, Tokyo, and Beijing. Of course, these were all cities that—according to Elite history books—no longer existed.

At any rate, Tazh Khan's men obviously weren't comfortable with Vlosk, or probably even with buildings; they stopped well short of the outskirts.

Khan rode on alone with Lucy and me to where a classic Russian motorcar was waiting to take us to our transport.

I gave my pony an affectionate pat as I jumped down to the ground. I'd become fond of the little brute. It was tough, loyal, gave everything it had, and asked little in return.

Tazh Khan spoke a quick couple of sentences to Lucy, but his gaze was on me.

"He asks how your shoulder feels," she told me.

"Already better. I'm good," I said, rotating it easily. He'd taken the arrow out himself, then washed my wound and dressed it with the sooth-ing balm they used on their horses. My own rapid-healing powers had taken over from there.

Looking rather somber, Tazh Khan spoke again.

"He says he knows you deliberately let his arrow hit you," Lucy said.

"Tell him I mean no disrespect, but he's mistaken. His shot was so swift and sure that I barely managed to save my life."

When she relayed this, his grin appeared, even as he spoke. Lucy kept on translating.

"He says you're a bad liar but he'd be proud to call you his brother."

"The honor's mine," I said, and I actually meant it.

"After this war is over, you must come visit him again," Lucy said. "He'll lend you his fattest wives to keep you warm at night, and take you spear hunting for wolves."

Now it was my turn to grin. "Sounds like a dream vacation. Tell him—*no way.*"

Tazh Khan clasped my forearm, leaned down from his horse to embrace Lucy, then rode off to rejoin his band—without a backward glance.

"That is some kind of man," I said. "They all are."

Lucy nodded sadly. "Exactly the kind of barbarian the Elites can't wait to exterminate."

Chapter 61

IT TURNED OUT that most of the mining labor in Vlosk was robotic; there weren't many human inhabitants, and though they'd tried to add touches of warmth—brightly painted houses, for one thing; greenhouse gardens; a couple of rough-house taverns—the place was still as grim as an addict's funeral.

But our driver, a bristly-mustached young man named Sergei, seemed cheerful enough—maybe because, like the nomads, he wasn't living with the Elite boot pressed down on his neck.

Our flight was ready to depart, so we said a hasty good-bye to Sergei and drove with a robot attendant to a bulky transport missile waiting on one of the launchpads.

Trouble was, these ships didn't have passenger accommodations; there wasn't much demand for them. The few occasional travelers were sealed into small cargo units that were pressurized, heated, and oxygenated.

Lucy and I climbed into the one that was ready for us. It was about the size of a double coffin and just big enough to get us both in—not all that different from the trunk of her car, only with a little more legroom.

After the jolts and metallic clamor of final loading and the fierce roar and terrific acceleration of blastoff, everything settled down into a deep, dark silence.

Lucy and I lay there side by side, close enough to touch, but *not* touching.

I could hear her breathing though. And I was surprised that she wore some kind of fragrance. She must have put it on before getting into the cargo space. Was the perfume for me?

"Just in case you're getting any ideas, *don't*," she said after a minute.

"Farthest thing from my mind. Hadn't occurred to me."

"Oh, really? It didn't look very far from your mind when I found you in your car yesterday, making out with your dream girl."

I could feel my face redden. "I can't help what happens when I'm asleep."

"Asleep!" she said scornfully. "You had the simulator on full blast."

"I was just trying to relax. So I could *get* to sleep."

To my surprise, she giggled. "You didn't look very relaxed. Or sleepy either. You seemed rather alert."

I didn't have any snappy comeback to that, so I decided to go on the offensive.

"You're the one who started a striptease for those bush pilots. Pardon the pun."

"It was just business," she said with the patience of a teacher speaking to a child. "Yuck— I just got your joke about the pilots."

"That's all it is for you, just business?" I demanded. "You're the iron maiden?"

This time she sighed, a sound that might have been troubled, or just bone tired.

"No," she said. "Not iron, and not a maiden either. Get some sleep, *brother*."

"I definitely will," I said. "By the way, you smell nice. For a human."

"Thank you," Lucy said. "Pig."

"No — *skunk*."

Chapter 62

WHEN THE ORE ship finally landed—presumably in England, imagine *that*—I waited impatiently for the lid of our cargo unit to slide open and let us out. British allies would be there to meet us and take us on to London, a city I'd read about in countless books—books by Dickens, Austen, Amis, Smith, Maugham, Lodge.

I wasn't expecting to be greeted with tea and crumpets—but I certainly wasn't expecting what did happen.

The shipping unit was suddenly flipped upside down, dumping us into a mesh net, just as if we were a couple of fish.

Instantly, several threatening rifle barrels held by tight-lipped Brit soldiers were thrust in my face.

"What is this? What's happening now?" I snapped at Lucy. "More lies?"

"Be calm, Hays. Be patient, please. No one is going to harm us."

"Don't even twitch, Baker," one of the soldiers commanded in a crisp English accent.

Twitch? I was flooded with rage. How dare they treat Lucy and me in such a disrespectful manner!

"They're just suspicious. They want to question you, but I couldn't tell you that," Lucy admitted. "I was afraid you'd—"

"Do something stupid?" I said. "Like maim several of them? Which I *could* do."

The rifle barrels poked at my stomach and chest.

"You heard the major," a sergeant growled. "Shut your mouth."

"He said not to *twitch*," I corrected the insolent soldier.

"Please, just go along," Lucy urged. "I'm sorry, but there's no way around it, Hays." She really did seem apologetic, for what that was worth. *Not very much.*

"Come along, miss," the major said to Lucy.

"Sir Nigel wants to see you straight off." He led her away, leaving me alone with my new group of pals.

"They tell us you're some kind of poofter wonder boy," the sergeant sneered. "We'll have to see about that."

"Let me guess—you have ways of making me talk," I cracked. "And I'm supposed to come back with 'Do your worst!' Right?"

Clearly these lads were not chosen for their keen senses of humor. They stared at me stonily.

"Yeah, that'll about cover it," the sergeant said.

Chapter 63

I COULD SEE why the humans would want to be careful with me, but still . . .

"You expect us to believe that for all those years you could carry on as Mr. Super Elite Agent— without anyone there having an idea there was somethin' *off* about you?" the interrogator said with professional menace in his voice.

He'd asked me that same question, one way or another, at least a dozen times in the past hour— which was about how long I'd been hanging from the ceiling of a room in a military jet somewhere over southern England.

To be more precise, I was inside a mesh net, which they'd hoisted up so my feet didn't quite touch the floor. A thin metal bar had been inserted under my crotch, and I was forced to straddle it with my full weight.

Damned uncomfortable, and not very hospitable of the Brits.

"It's like being a bit *thick*," I said. "You don't know it until somebody tells you."

I could see the interrogator bristle at the insult, but he kept concentrating on the monitor of the brain analyzer they had me hooked to— a sophisticated lie-detection device that I knew was close to infallible.

Once again, he shook his head unhappily at what he saw. He turned to a Brit major who was standing by and observing me like I was a ticking bomb, which wasn't entirely wrong.

"Never come across a reading like this before, sir," he said. "Not a termite—but not exactly human either."

Termites, I'd gathered by now, was what European humans called Elites—probably a slam at their unimaginative, orderly minds.

"Could I offer a helpful word, gentlemen?" I said. "I'm very familiar with this kind of equipment—I suspect the problem's *in the machine*."

I wouldn't have believed it possible for a man's jaw to get any tighter than the interrogator's already was, but it did.

"This machine is excellent," he said. "Top of the line. Nothing but the best for testing the likes of you."

"Have you ever used it in this aircraft? Or any aircraft at all?"

He hesitated — then, under the major's steady gaze, said, "And your point would be?"

"The alpha-wave regulators are extremely sensitive to destabilizations of ionic-bombardment levels," I said. "Even a slight change of environment can knock the whole operation out of sync. Taking it to this altitude and speed is like throwing it into a subatomic waterfall."

"Well, Sandor? What do you say to that?" the major asked. "The man has a point. Destabilization of ionic-bombardment levels, hmmm?"

"I can prove it," I said. "Hook yourself up to it. Check your own brain patterns as a reference. They might not be exactly *normal,* but I assume you know what they look like."

"Do as he says," the major commanded. "Do it at once. I want to see this."

Grimly, the interrogator affixed a wireless headset to his own temples, connecting himself to the apparatus.

And also to me.

I stayed still for thirty seconds, concentrating all mental energy in the atrium of my brain's implanted computer chip—the mechanism that allowed control over my body's involuntary functions.

Then I blasted a pulse outward—an electro-magnetic shock wave moving literally at the speed of thought.

The monitor's screen shattered with a *crack,* and the interrogator's feet left the floor by a good six inches. His bulging eyeballs looked like they were blistering on the inside. The headset smoked against his temples.

In the stunned silence that followed, the room's door opened and Lucy stepped in, along with a well-dressed older man.

He glanced appraisingly at the half-melted equipment and the lurching, drooling interrogator.

"Point taken, Agent Baker," he said. "Major, set this man free. He's an ally. And a friend of Megwin's."

Chapter 64

AND STILL, THE carefulness persisted. Or was it just human paranoia at this point? Hard to distinguish between the two sometimes.

"So that wretched psychopath President Jacklin actually told you of a plan to wipe out humankind?" said Sir Nigel Cruikshank—the man who had ordered my release and the chief of Britain's top intelligence agency, the MI7. He had a deeply lined, world-weary face and a sense of tough integrity. He'd already apologized for his soldiers' rough treatment of me, but I countered that their suspicion was understandable, and actually prudent.

I respected Sir Nigel instinctively, and I was

already starting to like him. Imagine that, *me liking a human.*

"Jacklin used the phrase 'making the world a safer, cleaner place,' but that's not what he meant," I said.

"But he gave no indication of how this would happen? Or when, Hays?"

"Actually, no. I assumed he was talking about a military attack. A big one."

"I see," he said, pronouncing it somewhat like *I say.*

He walked to the rim of the ancient stone tower of Old Sarum, which we were standing atop, and leaned his forearms on the wall, gazing out over the wide expanse of Salisbury Plain.

Lucy and I followed him. A team of armed guards followed *us* everywhere, although now — supposedly — they were here for our protection.

"Are you thinking the plan is something different?" Lucy asked Sir Nigel.

"We're preparing for a full military attack, of course. Monitoring their troop movements and readying our own forces. But something about it just doesn't feel right to me."

"How so?" I asked.

"Hard to explain, Hays. I've spent long years going point-counterpoint against the Elites—in older times, it was called a 'cold war.' Got to know their ways quite well.

"Now I just can't rid myself of the sense that what they're doing is too obvious, even for their tidy minds. I don't believe they want anything resembling a fair fight. They're very cerebral, and totally ruthless. The Elites have zero respect for human life. We're skunks, insects, ciphers. As you well know, Hays."

"I'm sorry I can't help more," I said. *"But I am here to do what I can."*

"It's fine, Hays. Well, have a good look 'round. That's why I brought you here."

He waved a hand toward a military installation that was visible in the distance—a large complex of buildings, airfields, missile launchers.

"That base there is our defensive nerve center. You'll get to know our best people, our best minds. I happen to think they're the *world's* best minds: analytical, very creative, and, most of all, compassionate. The human race has come a long way since 7-4 Day. I hate to say it, but we're better because of it."

For the first time in my life, I was struck by the contrast between the ugly modern buildings and highways in New Lake City and these landmarks from the ancient past—the spire of Salisbury Cathedral piercing the sky and the fantastic pillars of Stonehenge. Like the Old Sarum tower, they weren't just beautiful, they were magnificent—and all built by human minds and hands, long before the sound of a machine had ever been heard. Amazing feats of architecture and engineering.

With Elites, newer and more efficient was always better, particularly with anything built before 7-4 Day. If they hadn't torn it down already, it was only because they hadn't gotten to it yet.

Sir Nigel swung around to face me.

"Hays, I *want* to believe in you—in the way I believe in Lucy—so I'm setting aside my usual caution," he said. "I'll be blunt as to why, and it's not flattering. I simply feel that we've reached a point where my people have nothing to lose. But I must bring up one more seriously troubling issue."

His eyes drilled into mine with a gaze that seemed older than the blunt stones we were standing on. This was the kind of lie-detector test that no machine could match. Face to face, eye to eye.

"Did you honestly have no idea that the chap you worked for, Jax Moore, was the driving force of the genocide on 7-4 Day?" he said. "That he personally planned and carried out the murder of millions of humans?"

It was another jolt, but my armor of numbness was getting thicker all the time.

Seven-four Day had happened before I was born, and I only knew what all Elite kids were taught — *that it was the great celebration of saving the world from human destruction, a glorious victory without any hint of cold-blooded massacre.*

As Elite children, we were also taught that all humans were savage and evil and, on a purely rational basis, hopeless.

"I trusted Jax Moore for years, then found out the hard way that he's a lying snake," I said bitterly. "I never heard anything linking him and 7-4 Day, but I can believe it. I *do* believe it. Jax Moore led the attack when my mother and father were murdered."

Not a muscle in Sir Nigel's face flickered, and

his eyes stayed locked on mine like all-knowing magnets.

"Then, of course, you also weren't aware that your charming wife, Lizbeth, was Jax Moore's main accomplice," he said.

There was no amount of armor that could hold *that* shock off. I stared back at Sir Nigel, my mouth opening in disbelief.

"Is—is this some kind of a trick?" I stammered.

"Nothing of the sort. I couldn't be more serious."

"But—it's *impossible!* It can't be true. She isn't old enough, for one thing."

"Quite easy to prove to you, I'm afraid. I have documented her actions myself. Lizbeth's much older than you think, Hays. Much, much older. Decades older."

What he saw in my face must have finally satisfied him, because he gave a grim little nod.

"Right, then," he said. "Let's get on to London. There are people waiting to meet you. You're seen as something of a savior there, lad. I sincerely hope that you are."

Chapter 65

WELL, I DEFINITELY knew that I wasn't a savior in any way, shape, or form. On the other hand, I'd been wrong about so much lately, and maybe there were more secrets about myself I still needed to learn.

At any rate, I was finally in London, and it was a gorgeous city, probably the most beautiful I had ever visited. Clearly, it had the most history.

"I could go for a stiff whiskey just now. Perhaps a double," Sir Nigel muttered as Lucy and I strode with him through a corridor in the famed Tower of London.

I could have used a stiff drink myself. I was *still* reeling from the bomb, true or not, that he'd dropped on me about Lizbeth. But I did my best to shake off the shock and get ready for the grilling I was about to receive from England's top government and military leaders.

The meeting chamber's massive wooden doors were guarded by a pair of the Tower's yeomen warders, in ceremonial uniforms and tall hats—which seemed slightly odd to me, if not downright silly. No matter what *I* thought, however. They stepped smartly aside, opening the doors, and Sir Nigel led us to the front of the room.

At least a hundred people were waiting in there, and heavily armed soldiers were stationed all around the perimeter.

Savior? I thought. *I don't think so, ladies and gents. Just another human being under a death sentence.*

"You all know by now that Hays Baker is the only human who has lived and operated as an Elite Agent of Change," Sir Nigel announced brusquely. "That and his extraordinary mental and physical abilities make him of immense value to us. So let us waste no time—"

Suddenly, the huge doors swung open again and four of the yeomen warders appeared.

But now they crouched in combat position—

255

leveling rifles they must have kept hidden in their baggy uniforms.

Could this be possible? Clearly, it was.

"Elites!" Lucy screamed, with the loathing of a woman shrieking "Rats!" in a four-star restaurant. The room instantly erupted in a spray of murderous gunfire. The British soldiers, taken by treacherous surprise, barely had time to swing their weapons into action before they were cut down in shameful numbers. The crowd of leaders, cursing and shouting, scrambled for cover where none was to be found.

I slammed my shoulder into Lucy and Sir Nigel, sending us all skidding across the floor into an alcove—a nanosecond or less before the wall where we'd been standing exploded in a hailstorm of dust and plaster.

"It's *you* they're after," Sir Nigel yelled. "For God's sake, run! We can't afford to lose you! You're the most important person in this room. *Run!*"

But there was no place to run *to*. The alcove was blind, without doors or windows, and the Elites had us pinned in there with their blistering cross fire.

Obeying Sir Nigel as best I could, I sprang up in a charge at the alcove's rear wall and crashed against it with all my strength. The old plaster was thick, but I punched on through to the next room—and rammed straight into a row of standing suits of armor.

The metalware went flying in all directions with a clatter like a truckload of cymbals dumped off a high-rise building.

Lucy was right behind me. "We have to jump!" She panted, yanking me to my feet, pointing toward a row of arched windows. "Don't argue. Don't think about it."

Just then, the Elites' laser bursts hissed around us, *spang*ing off the cascading armor and smashing glassed-in displays of ancient pikes and broadswords and such.

"Yes, sir, ma'am!" said I.

Chapter 66

SAVIOR? I DON'T think so. I doubted I could even save myself right now. And why should Elites consider me so undesirable—just because I knew some of their secrets? Or was it Lucy they were really after?

At any rate, Lucy went left and I went right, both of us diving headfirst through windows that were located only a few feet apart. We came down in a shower of glass, landing on opposite sides of a steep tile roof. Without pausing, I bounced off it and into a quad somersault, tucking and twisting to dodge the gunfire still flashing around us.

As I spun, I caught a glimpse of Lucy bravely leaping over the Tower's outside wall. A second later came the splash of her hitting the river far below.

Thank God—underwater was the safest place she could be right now.

The warders were still following us and shooting, their ridiculous hats sailing off in the breeze as they jumped out onto the roof. I leaped forward and landed on a turret wall, then I scuttled around to its far side.

Next, I threw myself backward off the turret in another long, twisting flip and landed on top of the Tower's outside wall, now facing the majestic Thames. I ran along the wall, sucking in air, straining to reach maximum speed.

The afternoon fog had turned to drizzle, and the surface of the huge bridge cable where I landed next was slippery with moisture. The awful sound of laser fire still hissed with menace in my ears.

But this was an acrobatic act that even the Elite assassins couldn't follow. If I succeeded.

I dashed across the bridge's top span and slid on my feet down the cable on the other side. I was like a kid on a snowboard—being shot at!

I finally saw Lucy again, dripping wet and running across the lower bridge past aston-ished motorists and a few stiff-upper-lipped Brit pedestrians.

"Don't even slow down," she shouted up to me.

"Couldn't if I wanted to!" I called back. Then I dropped thirty feet or so to the pavement and continued to follow her lead. I had no idea yet why she was so important to the resistance, but she had certainly been a lifesaver for me.

So far.

Chapter 67

SOMEHOW WE MANAGED to get to shelter at a high-priority safe house run by MI7, right there in London. I had wanted to see the House of Lords, Westminster Abbey, the Tate—maybe even take a train to Paris—but I was stuck in an apartment under armed guard.

"What's going on with you?" Lucy finally asked, clinking her fork onto her dinner plate. "You've got to be starving. But you're picking at your food like a weight-conscious canary. And you're looking at me like I'm the cat."

It was our second day in the safe house, an apartment somewhere near Hyde Park that had an anonymous facade in a block-long building row that looked just like dozens of others around it. But were we actually safe here?

I had no idea, but I doubted it. The Elites were definitely on our trail now, and they were very good at this kind of skunkhunt.

The inside of the apartment was spacious and nicely furnished, complete with a servant android—who reminded me of Metallico, except female, much more polite, and armed. The gun-toting robot had set out a curious spread of roast beef, mutton, vegetables, mashed potatoes, scones, and jelly. Plus, a stiff drink for each of us.

But my appetite simply wouldn't kick in, and I decided to speak my mind, even though it might create a breach between Lucy and me.

"Did you know about Lizbeth being in on 7-4 Day?" I asked. "You did, didn't you, Lucy? You knew all this time, but never told me?"

She kept looking at me steadily. "Yes, I'm afraid I did, Hays."

"So why didn't you tell me?"

"Because I knew Sir Nigel would want to handle it himself. He told me as much."

I set down my fork. Actually, I threw it at my plate.

"I'm sick to death of being jerked around,"

I said. "And you seem to be doing a lot of the jerking, *sister.*"

"I'm sorry, Hays, I truly am. But that's just the way things have gone so far. This is a crisis situation, no? It's not *me* who wants to deceive you."

"Got any more little secrets to share? I'd like to know all of them now."

"*Secrets?*" she said scornfully. "If you want to talk about trust, we have a lot more reason not to trust you than the other way around. You were an Elite bastard until very recently. You were, you *are*, married to Lizbeth."

Lucy stood up abruptly and stalked out of the room.

Well, that hadn't gotten me very far, had it? In fact, it had been a disaster. I wanted to make a bond with Lucy, but I kept messing up. We both did.

By now I'd had some time to think about Lizbeth. Part of me kept insisting that what I'd heard so far was impossible. To start with, she was two years younger than me—born *after* 7-4 Day.

Or had she been?

I'd met her twelve years ago in New Chicago, soon after I started working at the Agency of Change. About her past before that, I only knew what she'd told me. Of course, I'd seen the marriage documents listing her birth date. But documents could easily be altered... If Nigel's story was correct, she'd have to be at least twice my age. But Elites stayed youthful far longer than humans, and with the science work she did, she had access to the latest anti-aging technology.

I'd taken it for granted that Lizbeth loved me, but now I remembered her cold side. Everything in her life was chosen for maximum function and efficiency. And she had turned her back on me the instant my troubles started!

Was the woman I'd given my heart to really a cold-blooded, scheming monster? Had she devoted her earlier life to helping the Elites annihilate much of the human race?

Then what?

She had coolly decided she was ready to start a family, saw a promising young agent, and lied to him about everything you could lie to someone about. Even our marriage vows—had they been calculated lies too?

Others would have to have been in on it — but there *were* others, like Jax Moore.

My brain and gut were giving me the terrible news about my marriage: it had all been a rotten, stinking lie. *My entire life was one big lie.*

Chapter 68

SPEAKING OF DELUDING oneself—there were always amazing toys to play with, even in an MI7 safe house. I couldn't resist. No one can...

With eight seconds left in the World Cup soccer game, the score stood tied, one to one. The earth trembled under my running feet from the stamping of the hundred thousand screaming fans who packed the stadium.

I booted the ball up in a high, looping pass and charged down the grassy field to receive it back, racing fiercely against the other team—the past year's World Cup champion from Italy.

Twisting and feinting, I cut sharply in and out of the sprinting figures.

Then someone slammed into my legs and

knocked me rolling—one of the Italian players had blindsided me.

The crowd's roar rose to a fury and the ground shook like an earthquake—but the referee was acting like nothing had happened!

I came up off the ground in a footfirst lunge.

I saw the ball.

It had reached the top of its arc and hung there for an instant like the sun, then it quickly gained speed as it plunged downward.

I launched myself toward it—with every stitch of its black and white hexagons, every scuff and scrape on its surface, crystal clear in my vision.

The goalie leaped into position, his body tensed, arms spread wide.

I feinted at the ball with my head, but at the last second, I ducked, flipped, and smashed it with my foot toward the far side of the net.

The goalie spun to follow and made a desperate leap, but his fingertips only grazed it as the ball shot into the far upper corner.

Boom! The sound of the final gun.

The crowd turned into an insane human wave, tearing seats out of the stands, swinging them as they stormed the field.

Abruptly, the yelling voices and vivid colors disappeared, leaving a blank screen flashing the words "GAME OVER."

I tugged off my headset and sank back on the couch, panting, soaked with sweat.

This was one mother of a simulator! Everything had seemed so real.

Anyone who hid out here at the safe house had time on his hands. So MI7 made sure there was entertainment—Toyz Corporation's latest products. I'd been immersing myself in them, waiting for orders to come from Sir Nigel. Trying to keep my mind off Lizbeth and our kids.

Suddenly, a hand came to rest on my shoulder.

Slender.

Female.

Impossibly soft.

Tony red nails, long ones.

"Hi, Hays," said the house android, Anna. "I came to see if I could get you anything. Anything at all."

"I'm fine, thanks," I said, glancing at her distractedly. "Honestly, I am."

Then my head swung back for another look.

"Anna?"

I'd realized that Anna was no ordinary servant model. She was definitely high-end—not only intelligent, but also with the capacity to morph into other shapes.

Now she was wearing a slinky black dress with slingback high heels. Her eyes had turned liquid blue...and she'd developed a shock of blond hair. And I mean that—a *shock* of blond hair.

She could have been Lucy's twin.

"You like?" she asked.

Chapter 69

"BESIDES, AREN'T YOU getting bored with those silly-billy *simulated* games?" Anna continued, plopping down beside me on the couch. She smelled terrific too, with the same citrus fragrance Lucy wore sometimes. Like in the cargo unit from Russia.

She'd even adopted an excellent imitation of Lucy's voice. Now she kicked off her high heels and tucked her small feet under her shapely rear.

"Anna, you might want to consider a different role model," I suggested.

"If you say so, Hays. But I'm programmed to be very observant. I pride myself on it."

"What's that supposed to mean?"

"Oh, come on. There's so much tension between you two. You could cut it with…a butter knife.

Competitive. Sexual. Gender-bending. Anyone could see it. But enough about you and Lucy."

I bristled. Just what I needed—an android playing shrink. And being right.

"There is some tension, I guess," I said. "And plenty of good reasons for it."

"The main one is that you're very attracted to her. Admit it—at least to me. You're *hot* for Lucy."

"That's nonsense, Anna."

"I don't mean to argue with you," she said soothingly. "But how could it hurt to give *us* a whirl?" Anna changed positions and crossed her legs, the black dress hiking up to reveal a long expanse of absolutely perfect thigh. "This is my purpose in life, Hays. To give pleasure." She smiled. "Make an honest woman out of me."

I couldn't help smiling at that one. "Very cute."

"Yes, I am."

Anna glided gently up onto my lap. Her voice took on a silken tone. "I promise you, I'm a lot more fascinating than those simulator toys. I change with your mood, your every wish, your desires. I've been told that I'm the best in Europe."

I didn't have a problem believing that. Not

271

at all. Anna's warm body pressing on mine was starting to weaken my defenses.

Almost against my will, my hands began exploring Anna's new shape, and, along with her breathless gasps of pleasure, they confirmed my guess about her anatomical perfection. Anna was all woman, all over, all the time, all mine—if I wished.

She deftly unbuckled my belt, cupped my vitals, and slid my pants down. *Hoo boy!*

"I see I finally have your interest—up," she said. "My, my, Hays. You just might be the best in Europe yourself."

But sonofabitch if the front door didn't open just at that second—and in walked, of all people, *Lucy.*

She folded her arms, eyebrows rising, and leaned back against the wall.

"Well, well, now I know what I'd look like if I were a street whore," she said.

"It would be an improvement over your current pig-farmer style," Anna shot back.

Lucy seemed amused rather than angry. "Not bad, roboslut. But playtime's over. Sir Nigel wants to see your boyfriend. *Hays, pull up your trousers!*"

Chapter 70

A FEW MINUTES later, thoroughly chastened, I was in a speeding car with Lucy at the wheel. London continued to be a revelation to me, especially the tasteful blending of old and new architectural styles. This was such a refreshing change from monolithic New Lake City with its streamlined, very modern *everything*.

There was one disturbing similarity with the Elite world that I had known though: toys were all over the place. Both for children and adults.

"Plenty of those creepy little dolls around here. I guess a fad is a fad," I muttered as Lucy drove us through the outskirts of London. Little Jessicas and Jacobs seemed to be everywhere. One of their tricks was to wave at cars and their passengers. I didn't wave back.

"Look who's down on toys all of a sudden," Lucy said, giving me a sidelong glance and a chuckle. "You were having a pretty good time with one just a few minutes ago."

"Let's just look at the scenery, please... Now who, or what, are *they*?"

A gang of street punks, dressed all in black and carrying long iron crowbars, were hanging out on the corner ahead. When they spotted our official-looking car, they thrust their crowbars into the air, then tapped them menacingly against their palms. Very, very *West Side Story*.

"Smashers," Lucy said. "They're like Betas, except they specialize in destroying anything civilized: monuments, art, books, schools, museums, churches—of course—even cemeteries. The Elites pay them to do it, supply them with addictive drugs like wyre. That's another fad sweeping the world."

I nodded grimly. What she was saying would fit with the overall Elite plan—to degrade and demoralize humans in any way possible.

It was clear that they were succeeding too. While downtown London was well policed, parts of these outskirts looked shockingly like the human slums in New Lake City. We were the only moving vehicle in sight. The neighborhood people watched us with dull, wary faces.

The difference was that, back home, the ugliness stemmed from neglect and poverty. Here, as Lucy said, things of beauty were specifically targeted. The stained-glass windows of graceful old churches were bashed to splinters, stone walls were ruined by painted scrawls, park greens were ripped up by car tires, statues lay toppled, fountains and ponds were open sewers for waste and poisons.

The Smashers were always busy, earning their pay, having their fun.

The punks on the corner were starting to yell at us now, a monotone, three-syllable chant. *"Sticks and stones! Break your bones! Sticks and stones! Break your bones! Sticks and stones!"* Let me guess — *"Break your bones"*?

"They like to work people over with those crowbars — then hang them on hooks to die," Lucy said. "Their idea of a good time."

Suddenly, a bottle came flying toward the car provided to us.

My impulse was to jump out and feed it back to the scum who'd thrown it. I was armed now—the MI7 had given me a couple of compact pistols. But I reminded myself that Sir Nigel was waiting and we had to keep moving.

In the next instant, a second bottle exploded into a fireball, rocking the car from its wheelbase. A sheet of flame shot up beside my face. I could feel the heat through the closed window.

Another crude petrol bomb blew up ahead of us—then another. I swiveled around to look behind and make sure we were safe. We weren't. The gang of Smashers was racing toward us, howling like werewolves and waving their trusty crowbars. More of them were pouring out of nearby buildings.

We'd fallen into an ambush, hadn't we? There was no way we could make it through the alley ahead without the car being disabled—which would leave us on foot and at the mercy of this raging, hot-blooded mob.

"One eighty!" Lucy yelled in warning.

She stomped hard on the brakes and yanked

the wheel around to bring us into a screeching spin. I clawed one of my pistols free of its shoulder holster and lowered the window. I aimed into the teeth of the nearest charging punk. "Get back, get away!" I yelled. He didn't. He swung his crowbar at me instead.

I fired and his face dissolved, fragments of flesh and bone exploding like one of their petrol bombs.

I kept shooting as our wildly fishtailing car slammed into more of the screeching attackers.

"Watch out!" Lucy gasped, dodging as an iron bar bashed through the windshield. One of the Smashers had somehow gotten on the roof.

I threw open the car door, leaned out, and touched off a point-blank round that blew away the hitchhiker.

There must have been fifty more Smashers though, the nearest ones using their crowbars like grappling hooks to smash through windows and pull themselves up onto the car.

"Sticks and stones! Break your bones!" they screamed. As they swarmed onto the car like ants on a cricket corpse, rocking it to turn it over, Lucy pulled us out of the screeching U-

turn and rammed the accelerator to the floor. The car lunged forward, with me still hanging out the door and snapping kicks at several snarling Smasher faces.

A second later, the car lurched free of the howling mob and streaked away from their fiery trap, reaching one hundred miles per hour by the end of the block.

I jerked loose a crowbar that was jammed in a window and raised it in front of the two Smashers who were still hanging on like leeches.

"You have one thing right," I yelled. "Breaking bones is *fun!*"

They let go and tumbled away into the London fog.

Chapter 71

"I AM AFRAID that the invasion by the Elites, the premeditated annihilation, is almost upon us," Sir Nigel said. "I've decided you two must continue your operations elsewhere. I'm sending you to a location in France. An emergency meeting is in progress there now. Nothing could be more important. Perhaps nothing in our history has ever been more important."

The poor, maimed man was lying in a military hospital bed, and his speech was slow and labored, but still full of passion. During the Tower of London attack, Sir Nigel had been struck in the face and chest by laser fire. I had seen this kind of wound before. I knew he would die from it.

Lucy touched his arm lightly, her face tense

with concern. "I'm so sorry for your pain, sir. It's my fault. I brought Hays Baker to London."

"Nonsense!" Nigel raised his voice with visible effort. "It's essential that he's here with us. Hays Baker may be our only chance to survive this terrible ordeal. He and Lizbeth Baker. Seven-four Day was just a warm-up round for this abomination. This is the fault of that monster President Hughes Jacklin."

"When do we leave?" I said.

"That's the spirit. There's a stealth jet waiting for you now. You'll parachute into France. When you get to the world summit meeting, pay special attention to the memory-purge sessions. Remember—memory purge!"

"Have there been any breakthroughs?" Lucy asked anxiously. "Sir Nigel?"

"I know that our finest scientists are working on it—feverishly. Your recent contribution was a great help," he said to Lucy.

I glanced at her. "What contribution was that?"

"Elite brains," Lucy said, as calmly as she'd say *a box of chocolates.* "You remember those headless Toyz Corporation executives in Baronville?"

I'd hardly thought about that in the turmoil of the past days, but Lucy's words brought back shocking images of the executives.

"This is a *war*," Sir Nigel reminded me. "We are trying to stop a holocaust that could actually eliminate the human race. You must go to France, first. Then move on across Europe—Italy, Germany, the Netherlands, Sweden, and Norway. Then on to Asia—if there's time. Sound the warning loud and clear."

He offered his hand. I clasped it gently, and Lucy leaned over to kiss his cheek. We suspected that this might be the last time she and I would ever see Sir Nigel Cruikshank.

"*Bonne chance,*" he whispered as we left.

Chapter 72

THE MILITARY STEALTH jet shot across the English Channel like a dark arrow cutting through the heart of the night. Lucy and I sat at the plane's rear, both of us silent, brooding. We had plenty to think about, trying to prepare ourselves for whatever might be coming next: probably a world war.

"I have to make an important stop along the way," Lucy said, standing up abruptly. "Sorry I didn't tell you before, Hays."

I nodded, though not completely following her. "Where are we stopping?" I asked.

Then I saw that she was readying a parachute—and that the red jump light was starting to flash.

"I thought we were going to the southeast of

France," I said. Even at the jet's terrific speed, we couldn't have made it there already.

"*You* are. I have some other business to take care of first. I'll catch up with you as soon as I can. Godspeed. If there could possibly be a God. What was that old song—'God Bless This Mess'? I always liked that sentiment. Good-bye, Hays."

I stared at her in complete disbelief. "Wait a minute—you're just leaving me?"

"There's no time to explain a couple hundred years of European history to you. But don't worry, Hays. You'll be met at your drop zone."

"Met by who?"

"The éminence grise of Interpol."

"The *what*? The *who*?"

"The person behind the scenes who's the real power here in Europe. Hays..." She looked at me earnestly, and I thought she was about to tell me something important, or maybe even personal. For some odd reason, I wanted her to. But she only said, "I wish it didn't have to be like this. But it does. As Sir Nigel said, we're in a war. A war of the worlds. This is the Big One."

Lucy waved as she stepped into the jet's parachute airlock and the door slid closed. Ten seconds later, no more than that, it reopened with the chamber empty.

Strangely, I felt incredibly alone with her gone. Maybe I had begun to think of Lucy as my only link between two hugely different worlds, Elite and human. Or maybe I just enjoyed her company. She seemed to know about everything, and she could make me laugh, even at times when I shouldn't.

But I didn't have long to ponder Lucy and myself before my own jump light started flashing. I immediately sealed myself into the airlock. Seconds later, I tumbled out into the cold, dark sky and was batted around like a feather by the jet's furious turbulence.

The whipping air got less fierce as I raced farther in my plunge toward earth. At an altitude of approximately three thousand feet, I popped open the chute. There was the satisfying shock of the harness seeming to yank my body upward.

Now I had some control, and I was able to study the landscape below.

Far to the south, I could see the long, glittering curve of the Côte d'Azur and the black emptiness of the Mediterranean Sea. Eastward lay the majestic Alps—huge, craggy, and mysterious shadows in the moonlight.

And directly underneath me—an impossibly small circle of flares marked my target.

I started furiously working the parachute cords to make sure that I landed close by. I was completely trusting Lucy now—and the humans of course. That was still unsettling to me—trusting them. But what other choice did I have?

My acute night vision didn't pick up any signs of hidden enemies. Just a single vehicle waiting midway inside the circle of flares. It sure wasn't a military transport.

It was a limo.

And the éminence grise? Where was he? Inside this fancy car?

I glided to earth as silently and invisibly as a ghost, landing in a forest with the crisp scent of pines filling my nostrils and the ground beneath my feet softened by their duff. For a full minute, I stayed crouched there, listening and watching the long, shiny, silver vehicle.

There were no sounds other than the wind through the tree branches and the timid rustlings of a few small animals on their nightly quest for supper.

I eased down onto my belly and started moving toward the flares—and the mysterious car parked out in the middle of nowhere.

Chapter 73

WHAT IS THIS all about? Another absolutely insane adventure? More deep secrets? And why isn't Lucy here with me for these vital meetings?

The limo's side door was open, revealing a dimly lit interior that looked, well, like a luxury hotel room—complete with a spa bathtub, which just so happened to be bubbling cheerfully.

Someone was splashing around in it.

A *female* someone with long, dark hair pinned up neatly behind her head and a few damp strands trailing down her neck. One of her hands was just now soaping her creamy skin. I couldn't quite see the face yet.

I spent the next few seconds convincing myself that I was really seeing what I thought I was.

"I see you too," the woman said.

She turned my way and I saw that her face had an exotic, aristocratic beauty, with a fine, arched nose and almond-shaped eyes.

"Welcome to France, Hays," she said. Her voice was husky and accented; she pronounced Hays as *Hezz*. "My name is Chantal Dugare."

"I thought... I was supposed to meet the *emmy-nonce greese* of Interpol," I said.

"That would be me."

I stayed where I was. Surprised, a little confused, maybe intimidated as well.

"No need to be nervous," she said soothingly. "You are our honored guest. There are resistance soldiers nearby—to protect us if need be. To protect *me*, certainly. Please, come inside the car. Shut the door."

I exhaled, stood up, and walked to the limo. What the hell—if I was heading into a fatal trap, at least it was an extremely attractive one. A *honey trap*. Wasn't that what they used to be called?

The door slid closed behind me, and then the car's automatic pilot started us moving through the countryside, accelerating to a rapid but smooth speed.

"Beautiful night for a ride," I said.

"It is, isn't it? Champagne?" Chantal Dugare replied, waving toward a silver ice bucket on a stand.

"Not just now, thanks. Do you always bathe in your car?" I asked next, sitting warily on a velvet couch beside the sloshing tub.

"Quite often, yes, I do. It relaxes me, helps me think through difficult problems. And I'm very busy, so it saves time."

"It doesn't bother you to have an audience?"

"Where's the harm in it? It's an old custom of the French aristocracy actually. Louis the Fourteenth?" Then, with a little laugh, she added, "Besides, I wanted you to know—*I'm not hiding anything.*"

If Chantal Dugare was, it was very well hidden. The froth of the spa water blurred her body, but I could see its outlines. Very nice, those outlines of hers.

"But something puzzles me," she said. "I expected your partner to be with you. Lucy?"

"She's not exactly my partner," I said, hedging. *And she's not exactly my sister, either.*

"But you've been with her lately, *non?* When did you two part company?"

"Actually, she bailed out of the plane just before I got here. I have no idea why. I have no idea where she is now. I do know this: she has a mind of her own."

Chantal nodded. "How strange." Then she eased forward in the tub, still submerged to the rounded tops of her breasts. She crossed her forearms on the rim closest to me, resting her chin on her slender wrists.

"Tell me," she said, her big, brown eyes fixed on mine. "Do you trust Lucy?"

Was *this* a trap—or just French seduction? If I admitted doubts about Lucy, I was betraying her. If I lied to cover for her, I was betraying the human cause. Either answer and my loyalty could be suspect.

"I'd be crazy to trust anybody at this point," I said. "Including myself."

She sighed, shaking her head in exasperation. "You talk like a schoolboy who thinks he's quite smart. How very American of you."

"I think of myself as a hybrid—don't you think that's right?"

She sighed again. "I think—you are quite handsome, Hays. I wish we had a little more time to be together."

"I see, and was all this a test?" I asked.

"A test? Well, if it was, you failed, but with flying colors. I wasn't expecting a gentleman."

"Then we're even. I wasn't expecting a very beautiful woman in a bathtub."

I felt the limo slowing, and a chime rang softly. The road had narrowed to a winding one-lane path. Ahead in the distance stood a huge, old, stone château with warmly lit windows, surrounded by well-tended vineyards—acres and acres.

"We arrive at our destination," she said. "I must ask you to look aside while I dress. But first, would you *be* a gentleman and kindly dry my back?"

She tossed me a big, fluffy towel, then rose up out of the tub, turning away demurely.

I couldn't really claim to be a gentleman, but I didn't mind pretending. And I was definitely right about one thing—the éminence grise was very beautiful, from top to bottom.

"You are peeking, *non?*"

"I am peeking, *oui.*"

"Then you pass the test, Hays. You *are* human. Very much so."

Chapter 74

AS THE VERY clever and alluring Chantal Dugare and I walked into the imposing dining hall of the château, she clapped her hands sharply to quiet the guests—about two hundred of them, from what I could see, representing many nationalities, standing in groups and talking excitedly. Waiters bustled around with trays, serving food and fine wines. It looked like a classy, but otherwise quite ordinary, party.

Except that these were reputedly the most important leaders in the free world—gathered to try to keep humankind from being destroyed by a powerful race that despised them.

"Attention, s'il vous plaît," Chantal called out in her husky and cultured voice. "I bring you Monsieur Hays Baker. We are honored that you are here."

Before she could continue, a stern-looking military man strode forward. He saluted me, then leaned in close to Chantal Dugare and spoke rapidly. Her intelligent eyes widened with concern as she listened. *Now what the hell is happening?*

"We have just received distressing news that your former boss, Jax Moore, is in Europe right now," she translated. "This is very dangerous for us. That man is the devil himself! He is a war criminal. A beast among beasts."

"I must agree with that." I spoke to Chantal, but also to the crowd. "I know that devil very well. He's extremely efficient. If he's here, the final plan is already in motion."

"We shall see," said Chantal, who, surprisingly, didn't seem as alarmed as I was.

Other guests approached me, introducing themselves and thanking me for being here. More than one told me that they'd known my parents and loved them both dearly, and offered sympathy for their senseless deaths.

Chantal was at my side again. "You must eat, Hays. Please. Something tells me we will need much strength soon. We all will."

I shook my head. "I wish I knew more about the Elite plan. I *want* to help you in any way I can."

She patted my arm. "We have ways to make you talk." She laughed. "What I mean is, there may be things you know that you aren't conscious of. We have tests. But first—*eat!*"

She snapped her fingers to summon a passing waiter and took a canapé of crusted bread spread with thick paste. "Pâté de foie gras, with truffles. Heaven on this earth. You *must* have one, Hays."

The smell of the food had been filling my nostrils since we first came in; a blend of savory aromas had my stomach on alert.

But there was a small problem. I was used to eating like an Elite, and even thinking about food like this went against my upbringing and training.

"Do you have anything…without calories?" I said.

The people standing nearby stared as if I were a crazy person. Chantal merely laughed.

"In France, you *dare* to suggest such a thing as fine cuisine without calories? That is an Elitist nightmare we can hardly imagine! Just try *this*. Open your mouth! I command it!"

She held the pâté to my lips, and I reminded myself that I was, after all, in France. So I opened my mouth—and she popped in the canapé.

What a glory! It practically melted on my tongue with a rich, subtle complexity that positively thrilled my taste buds. I turned to the waiter, ready to devour his entire tray. "Yes, please, I'll have another."

Then my hearing caught a faint sound that no one else in the room could catch—a jet, heading toward us at what seemed a low altitude.

Lucy! The idea delighted me more than I would have thought possible.

Chapter 75

BUT THEN MY ears told me that there wasn't just one jet — there were several of them! Had the war begun already? Here in the French countryside?

I ran to a window just in time to see a wing formation come streaking in, dropping string after string of Elite paratroopers — so many that they completely blotted out the moonlit sky. This was not good; I knew what tough and skillful fighters these were...

Hell, I had been one.

An explosion rocked the château with a tremor that I felt shoot up through my feet and jar my teeth. More bombs came right behind it, shattering windows, raining glass on the guests. Then bursts of gunfire erupted as the

French guards met the Elite attack outside on the grounds.

I hurried back to Chantal, who was issuing orders into a handheld phone.

Before I got to her though, the two sets of doors to the dining room flew open.

Elite commandos came charging in, firing assault weapons into the cluster of human leaders. It was a massacre of immense proportions.

Horrifying. Unthinkable. Cruel and unnecessary. None of these people were even armed.

Behind the waves of commandos walked a man and a woman, side by side, smiling as if they had just been announced at a fancy ball.

Jax Moore and Lizbeth!

"Great job, Hays," Moore called to me. "You led us right to the château—and handed us the kingpin. Or should I say, the *queenpin?*"

Chantal straightened her back and strode toward me. With a look of hatred like I'd never seen before, she slapped my face, raking her nails across my cheek. "Traitor! Pig! Bastard!" she screamed at the top of her voice.

Still smiling, Lizbeth calmly raised a pistol and shot her through the left breast. Chantal spun away, clutching at her heart, and fell like a beautiful bird torn from the sky.

Book Four

TOYS, TOYS, TOYS FOR ALL
GOOD LITTLE GIRLS AND BOYS

Chapter 76

HAYS BAKER IS no Elite! He's human … human … human …

I came awake thrashing, and very confused, as those ridiculous and awful words repeated over and over in my mind.

It took me a couple of seconds to realize that I was actually in my own bed. In my own apartment in New Lake City.

I'm safe. I'm home, aren't I? What in hell happened to me? I can't remember anything.

Lizbeth must have heard me—she hurried in to sit beside me, smiling indulgently, and gave me a warm kiss on the lips. The kiss was just what the doctor ordered. *The head doctor?* I wondered.

"Darling, I'm so glad you're with us again!"

she said. "How do you feel? The doctor said you would be more yourself today."

"OK, I guess. Except my brain feels like it's wrapped in a soaking wet towel. That can't be good, can it? What happened to me, Jinx?"

"You were badly hurt, Hays. Don't you remember crashing off the roof of that parking garage? You could have died along with the skunk on the motorcycle. They had you healing in a regeneration chamber until last night."

"*That fall with the motorcycle skunk?* That's what I'm recuperating from? How long was I unconscious? I don't remember much of anything. Sweetheart, I'm really confused. Terribly so."

"You were in a coma . . . for about a week. Since then you've been in and out of consciousness." She stroked my sweat-dampened forehead, but then withdrew her hand, wrinkling her nose slightly. "You do need a shower though. Sorry, Hays."

The queen of neat and clean—that was my Lizbeth. But in a strange way, I had missed that. At least it meant she cared.

"Now tell me everything. What *do* you remember?" she asked. "I've been on tenterhooks waiting to hear. Start at the beginning, Hays."

I shook my head, trying to pin down my blurred recollections. *The beginning?* When was that? Where was that? I had no idea, really.

"The Toyz store in Baronville—those ugly murders," I finally said. "I caught one of the killers on a motorcycle. We went off the roof of a parking garage, fell several stories, and crashed.

"Then the hospital, and the surgeons putting me under. Putting Humpty Dumpty back together again."

"Nothing after that?" she said, seeming oddly pleased, maybe because I was joking a little about the past.

"Well"—I managed a laugh, but it was shaky—"I did have this incredible nightmare about the doctors saying I was *human*."

"How awful for you, Hays. How bizarre." She tilted her head in sympathy, and truly seemed more beautiful than ever. "You poor, poor dear. But those kinds of hallucinations can happen with anesthesia, and sometimes they reflect bizarre fears. Do you have bizarre fears, darling?"

"No, I don't think so. But thank you, Dr.

Freud. I feel better already." I really did. "What happens now? When do I go back to work?"

"Moore wants you to come see him at headquarters as soon as you're up to it. Meantime, since you're feeling better…" Lizbeth's eyes got mischievous and very seductive. I certainly remembered *that* look—and very fondly. "Do you remember anything from *before* you went to the Toyz store that night?"

"Like what?"

"Like…that you and I had plans for a little private rendezvous, a little *us* time, until we were so rudely interrupted by the human miscreants?"

"Oh, yes! I do remember something about that." I placed my hand on Lizbeth's leg. I leaned in close and nuzzled her cheek.

"It just so happens that we're alone right now. Metallico took the girls to a birthday party for one of their friends. So why don't you go have that shower? I'll break out a couple of Rapture pills, and we can pick up where we left off. If you're up to it?"

"Honey, you sure know how to welcome a guy home," I said.

She kissed me again. Softly at first, then much harder.

"You're not just any guy, Hays. You're a hero. You're my hero. Now go wash up, in all those hard-to-reach places especially. I love you, Hays Baker."

Chapter 77

MY *WELCOME HOME* in the arms and breasts and long legs of my beautiful, violet-haired Lizbeth was certainly a memorable occasion. And it was heightened to the maximum by the Rapture we took—a legal drug for Elites only that produced an hour of euphoria and enhanced sensations such as "elevation," not to mention up to half a dozen orgasms, for each of us, of course.

There is nothing like having orgasm after orgasm, especially with somebody you love. Lizbeth and I climaxed separately, but also jointly, almost perfectly in sync. Rapture is a drug that definitely lives up to its name. Most authors complain that the pleasure is almost impossible to put into words, and I certainly agree with them.

Toys

Afterward though, Lizbeth got a bit edgy, certainly in no mood for the tender lounging around that I required. "What's the matter, Jinx?" I asked her.

"Oh, nothing really. But Hays, I do have to go to a meeting at the Agency. A quick one," she said, finally jumping out of bed. "I'm sorry, darling. Don't hate me for it."

She pulled fresh clothes from drawers and her closet, then hurried off to the shower. She stayed in there a long time.

When she came back to the bedroom, she was dressed in black-on-black business attire, but looked gorgeous as always. She also seemed—I don't know—brittle. Just a little out of sorts, hopefully not with me.

"What's wrong?" I asked. "Was it me? It was, wasn't it? I didn't perform as—"

"The girls will be home soon," she said. "I've shielded them from—you know—the harsh realities of all this confusion. The coma, your healing process."

"Of course," I said. They didn't need to know how I could have died crashing off that roof with the motorcycle assassin.

James Patterson

"And one more thing, darling. The nightmare you had...about the surgeons saying you were human? Little quirks like that...might keep cropping up for a while. Just recognize them for what they are, and tell me. It will help to talk them out. I'm here for you, Hays."

Still in the doorway, she blew me a kiss, then she left. "Love you," she called. "I miss you already."

I sighed, but then I smiled. I missed her too. My Jinx.

Chapter 78

I GOT OUT of bed, pulled on some clothes, and went to the kitchen to make myself a cup of high-protein coffee. My mind was still fuzzy, but that was understandable after lying unconscious for days. All in all, I was satisfied that I felt as good as I did. I'm thankful that I heal as fast as I do. All Elites do, but I seem particularly fortunate in that respect.

A few minutes later, I heard the front door open, and I rushed to meet my daughters, throwing open my arms, missing them even more than I thought I had.

"Chloe, April!" I cried. "Now...*which one of you is which?*"

But instead of laughing and hurling themselves

into my arms as I'd hoped, they stayed where they were, their little faces subdued. Metallico, the sassiest robot on the planet, stood behind them, as rigid as a tree.

I was absolutely stunned into silence. Something was very wrong here.

"What? No big hug for Daddy?" I finally managed a few words.

That brought Chloe and April to me—reluctantly—for a quick embrace. But then they pulled away. It was as if they barely knew me.

"We missed you," said April.

"Missed you," echoed Chloe.

Then the two of them shared a look and hurried off to their room and all their books and toys.

I turned to Metallico. "What's going on?" I said. "What am I missing here?"

"Going on, sir?" he replied with the formality of a butler in a palace, *someone else's* palace. "I don't know what you mean. No idea. Now if you'll excuse me, I have duties to attend to." The huffy robot marched stiffly past me toward the kitchen.

Sir? Metallico had never called me that before. He'd always treated me like an equal—at best.

So I followed Chloe and April to their room. I found them playing with Jessica and Jacob dolls. Lizbeth must have given in and bought them while I was gone. I just hoped they weren't the adult versions. Even these dolls looked at me funnily.

"Are you mad at Daddy?" I asked. "Did I do something I'm not aware of?"

They shook their heads, but neither girl spoke a word to me. Nor did the thoroughly creepy dolls.

"So what's the matter with you two gremlins? You don't seem glad to see me."

Chloe, my four-year-old, squirmed uncomfortably. "Mommy said something really bad happened to you. She said—"

"She said we're *not* supposed to talk about it," her older sister—age six—interrupted. "We're just glad you're all right, Daddy. We feel nothing but love and admiration for you. You're a hero."

"You're a hero!" mimicked Jessica and Jacob.

Lizbeth had probably been worked up when she explained things to our daughters, and they'd sensed her tension more than they'd heard what she actually said. Now they were just afraid. Temporarily, I hoped.

Or maybe all this strange behavior was just in my own mind—part of the anesthesia hangover.

"Something bad did happen to me. An accident," I told the girls. "But it's all over, and I'm fine. What do you want to do now? How about if I whip us up some"—I paused, frowning—"banana splits." What I'd started to say was *no-cal* banana splits. Where had *that* odd thought come from? Of course the treats would be no-cal. All Elite food was. Only human food was...

"Then we could play 3-D Monopoly," I said. "Or whatever you want. We can even play with your dolls." *Creepy critters that they are.*

"I'd like to play with Daddy," said Jessica with a leer. "Play with me, Daddy?"

Then Metallico came into the room with a silent, gliding walk that I'd never seen before. It was downright eerie, actually.

"The girls have had a busy day," he said. "My instructions from Lizbeth are to see to it that they have their baths, then their homework, and some much needed rest."

I didn't like any of this, but I accepted that my judgment was probably shaky. I decided to let it go. "All right then—brush and flush!" I said to the girls.

"But first, one more hug. For good luck, for good measure, and just for fun!"

Slowly, Chloe and April came to me and granted their dad a hug. But then April said, "Good luck, Daddy," and it sounded like she really meant it, like she knew I needed some luck.

"Good luck, Daddy!" chimed in Jacob and Jessica.

I wandered around the apartment after I left the girls, trying to get interested in the adult simulators and other toys of my own. But I was restless, I guess. I'd been cooped up inside long enough, hadn't I? Maybe that was the problem.

A good, hard run would be just what I needed to get back to normal, to be Hays Baker once again.

Chapter 79

WHEN LIZBETH ARRIVED at the sparkling glass palace known as Agency Headquarters, the atmosphere was more celebration than anything resembling regular police business. In fact, two dozen of the Elite government's highest-ranking officials were gathered in the main briefing room, sipping wine and cocktails. The conversations were charged with giddy anticipation of 7-4 Day.

Jax Moore met her as she came in and took her aside. "What's the update on Hays?" Moore asked quietly as he held a trademark cigar aloft.

"Exactly what we want it to be, Jax: he thinks everything's the same as always. He believes his hospitalization and healing followed his fall with that skunk motorcycle rider. He has no memory whatsoever of Europe. There was a blurred memory of voices overheard saying he was human, but I got him settled down."

A smooth smile eased across Moore's chiseled face. "I can imagine."

Lizbeth smiled back archly. "*You* don't have to imagine, do you, Jax?"

"You did your duty. Well done. President Jacklin will be very happy," Jax Moore said then. "Now we send him after his half sister, and no matter which one kills the other, we win."

Her smile stayed, but the slightest trace of unhappiness came into her eyes. "Of course we win. Elites have been winning every battle for thirty years. How else could this turn out?"

Moore didn't seem to notice Lizbeth's slight frown. "You're the bright star tonight, Lizbeth," he said. "Let's get you a drink, then it's time for you to take a bow. This augurs well for 7-4 Day."

He snapped his fingers and an obsequious robot waiter hurried over to offer her a perfectly made martini. Then Jax Moore turned to address the other guests. Their talk stopped, and everyone watched expectantly.

"As you know very well, we don't usually hold

Agency briefings in the form of cocktail parties," he began, then waited for a ripple of laughter to quiet. "But this isn't an ordinary occasion. It's really a *surprise* party — except the surprise isn't for us.

"On the coming 7-4 Day, our human neighbors are going to get the biggest surprise the modern world has ever seen. My friends, in just eighty hours, the human race will be completely eliminated. The greatest threat the earth has ever known will be gone. Hear, hear!"

"It has been a long time coming," Lizbeth added. "*Too* long."

Another excited murmur rose from the audience — the closest these reserved Elites ever came to cheering, or any such show of emotion.

"Let me add that we owe much of our upcoming success to the genius of this lady," Moore went on, draping an arm around Lizbeth's shoulders. "A toast to Lizbeth Baker — as brilliant as she is beautiful. No one has sacrificed more."

Glasses clinked together like chimes, and there was a chorus of hearty congratulations.

Lizbeth raised her own glass in gracious acknowledgment and flashed another brilliant smile. But then she moved quietly out of the limelight, to have a moment alone. The thrill she should have felt was smothered by the distress that was tightening her stomach. She lived by her steely intellect, and she scorned people who were soft in any way. But now she'd fallen into that sort of mess herself, hadn't she?

She wasn't bothered in the least by wiping out the nauseating human race. They were no more than insects to her—*or worse*—and the sooner they were eliminated from earth, the better for everyone, perhaps even for the humans themselves.

But tonight underscored what *was* troubling her: *Hays was the problem*.

When she'd first learned that he was human, she was, of course, outraged. She'd vented by making him a pawn against his own kind—then blocking his memory of those events. One way or another, he'd be dead in a matter of hours— loving husband and father, genuine hero for the cause, a man who had enriched her life in countless ways. The sense of loss was already cutting deep, and there was nothing her intellect could do about it. Dammit, she still loved Hays, didn't she?

Shake it off, Lizbeth! she told herself fiercely. *Hays is pitiful—a human.*

As she started to rejoin the crowd, a hand patted her from behind. She turned and looked into the face of the hulking McGill—Hays's former partner and friend. He was smoking a cigar, just like his mentor, Jax Moore.

"So what's it like jumping in the sack with a skunk?" McGill cracked, leering at her breasts as he always did. He'd obviously had far too much to drink already.

"We need to keep him happy as long as he's useful. Until 7-4, certainly," Lizbeth answered coolly. "I do what I have to—it's called being professional. It's my duty."

"Let me know when you're ready for the real thing—with another professional."

I'd sooner sleep with a baboon was her first withering thought—a comparison that wasn't far off. But then again, what better way to take final revenge against a husband who had weakened and confused her totally?

"Well, a *widow* may need consoling," she said and, for the first time in days, smiled in a way that felt genuine. Her true self was taking charge again: logical, selfish, brutal when necessary.

"I'll be there for you," said McGill, and then he added, "It's my duty too, and I'm very good at it. I'm all Elite, Lizbeth."

She laughed at that one—and lit up her own cigar.

Chapter 80

I LEFT MY apartment in a slight daze and walked the short distance to a favorite running path along the winding, and quite beautiful, Imperial Lake.

I busied myself stretching and limbering up along the way. Then I took off, going easy at first—testing myself to find out if I was more weakened than I thought.

But my body felt better than I had any right to expect, and I cranked up my speed until I was flying along in smooth, ten-yard strides.

There was hardly any traffic along the narrow lake road—one of the reasons I liked it here. A delivery vehicle with the logo of Ultima Medical Supplies zipped past me, and a few minutes later,

I saw that it had pulled into a service area ahead.

When I got there, the driver was leaning into the rear door, struggling with what appeared to be a large machine for delivery.

I slowed to a trot. "Need help?" I called. This was the kind of thing that Lizbeth hated about me—what she called my "mindless do-gooder impulses."

"Would you mind? Damn thing slipped off its tracks," called the driver—a female worker, as it turned out.

Her voice set off a tiny tick in my mind—like maybe I'd heard it before. But the sound was muffled, and where could I have run into this particular delivery person? I dismissed the thought as another one of my recent quirks, exactly what Lizbeth had warned me about.

As I walked closer, she hopped inside the vehicle and began moving her fingers expertly across the machine's controls. As I looked on, the machine came to life with little clicks and whirs, the monitor readouts flashing.

"That's an impressive piece of equipment," I said. "What's it do?"

"Oh, it's an ultrasound scanner—uses sonic

waves to destroy foreign objects in the body, like kidney stones or blood clots," she answered.

Then the delivery person swung around and looked straight at me.

"Or the tracking chip that effing Lizbeth planted in your brain," she said. "Hello, Hays."

Chapter 81

IN THAT INSTANT, I recognized both the face and the voice. She was the *terrorist* who'd led the attack on Lizbeth and me after the president's party.

I lunged toward her—but an electronic jolt slammed into my eyes and immediately pierced through to the back of my skull.

Then came a loud *pop,* and I felt as if I were getting smashed with a hammer on the *inside* of my head.

I spun away in agony, clutching my temple. Then I felt *her* hands catch my shoulders.

I managed clumsily to grab hold of her, determined to take her down too.

But the female terrorist didn't fight or pull

away—just held on to me, almost in an embrace.

"Calm down, Hays," she soothed. "You'll be all better in a few seconds. Trust me."

When she spoke my name, a powerful whirlwind of images erupted in my memory—all the things that had *really* happened during the days when I thought I'd been lying unconscious in an Elite hospital. Stunned and confused as I was, I understood immediately.

"*Lucy?*" I said hoarsely.

Chapter 82

"OF COURSE IT'S me. Are you strong enough to stand on your own?" she asked. I nodded, and we moved apart.

Like she'd promised, the viselike grip of pain in my skull was easing, and my thinking seemed clearer already. Suddenly, I remembered a whole lot of things that had happened after the motorcycle crash—Russia, England, France, Lucy, the murder of my parents by Jax Moore.

"Lizbeth planted a chip in my brain?" I groaned, lowering my face into my hands. "Is that true, Lucy? Careful now, I don't think I can handle too many more lies."

"Poor Hays. I started suspecting the worst when the Elites kept following us, and the MI7 confirmed it during that phony interrogation in London. That's why Sir Nigel sent you to the meeting in France."

"What?" I jerked my head up and stared at her. "He wanted to get the resistance leaders killed? That's insane, Lucy. Even if there is a war going on."

"Take it easy, Hays. He wanted the Elites to *think* they're dead," Lucy said. "So we set up a ruse, a very clever one. Those were just clones at the château. No one died. The real leaders are in hiding, and still hard at work. Desperate measures for desperate times. This *is* a war—to the death. Hopefully, not ours."

I exhaled slowly, trying to grasp all that I was hearing now. I'd suspected Lucy of treachery at first, but the real informant was *me*. And Sir Nigel had played me like a piano. As an ex-agent, I had to admire that—but the thought of the massacre still made me clench my teeth until they hurt. It helped a little to know the real Chantal Dugare wouldn't die loathing me.

And now—what?—the Elites had used another chip to block out my memory of the recent past? I should be honored, I suppose. They'd gone to a lot of trouble—sophisticated technology, careful planning, and the deceit they were carrying on now. Lizbeth had even used sex to lull me, and with her obvious disgust for humans, she must have forced herself back into our bed. No wonder she'd seemed edgy after half a dozen orgasms.

"They've got another use for me," I said. "That's why they're still playing me."

"So do we, Hays." Lucy's gaze was apologetic but intense. "Sorry, but that's what you get for being who you are."

"Mr. Popularity," I muttered. "So what do *you* want me to do now? How may I serve?"

"Just go along with them, Hays, like your memory's still blanked out. We need to find out *how* they plan to strike. We're pretty sure it won't be militarily. Sir Nigel now believes that those preparations in the field are a smoke screen. The annihilation of the human race won't involve hand-to-hand combat."

I shook my head hard, still trying to clear it. "I was just getting used to being a double agent. Now I'm what — a triple agent?"

Then Lucy surprised me by grasping my hands in hers.

"Hays, you have to be ruthless from here

on. Everything, and I mean *everything*, depends on making them believe you still think you're an Elite." Her grip tightened. "No matter what happens, keep reminding yourself: if they win, we're all dead. You too."

Strangely, I couldn't find any words to speak. I was lost in the sudden awareness that I'd never looked into eyes that were so clear and sincere. So human, I suppose.

Lucy finally lowered her gaze and let go of my hands. "I've got to keep moving. There are police all over—looking for me. I'll try to stay in touch. If it doesn't work out that way, well, you turned out to be pretty great."

With that said, she slammed the truck's rear door shut, jumped into the driver's seat, and then took off.

I started back toward home, still shaken by the recent burst inside my head—and much more disturbed by what I'd just learned about dear, sweet Lizbeth.

But by the time I got back to our apartment, my shock was overpowered by anger. At least I knew what side I was on now.

Hays Baker is no Elite! . . . Hays Baker is human!

Chapter 83

THE NEXT MORNING—a whole lot worse for the wear and tear—I walked rather purposefully into Agency Headquarters for my "welcome back" meeting with Jax Moore. My step was springy, and I greeted my old coworkers cheerfully—fighting the urge to start shooting each and every one of them on sight. These heart-less bastards were part of the brain trust behind a genocide plan. And so was my wife.

"It hasn't been the same around here without you," Moore said, welcoming me into his office with his usual ruggedly handsome smile and a handshake firm enough to break bones. I shook off the impulse to break all the bones in his face.

"I think we can get back on track pretty quick, boss," I said crisply, lying through my teeth.

"Coffee, Agent Baker?" asked the familiar mechanized voice of the office's built-in catering unit.

"The usual, thanks," I said, since I was being careful to make sure that "the usual" was exactly the impression I made.

Within seconds, a robotic arm handed me a cup of delicious espresso, strong and bitter. At least this stuff wasn't washed out like the no-calorie food served everywhere else in New Lake City.

Moore waved me to a leather easy chair and sat behind his all-glass desk. He lit up a stogie, and I kept imagining it blowing up in his face. *Seriously* blowing up.

"I've got a top-priority assignment," he said. "I wanted to give you a little time to rest, but it can't wait any longer. Hays, we need you. President Jacklin has asked for you personally. Are you feeling up to a little action?"

"One hundred percent," I said.

"Good—you're going to love this." He touched a control, and a monitor screen blinked on.

It displayed a life-size image of Lucy's face. I did, in fact, *love it.*

"Recognize her?" Moore said.

"She's one of the terrorists—the ones who attacked Lizbeth and me when we were leaving the president's party," I said grimly, as if my hatred of her was still fresh in my mind. But my guts twisted as I guessed what was coming next.

"She goes by the code name Lucy, or sometimes Megwin. How folksy those humans are," Moore said. "She's very good at eluding surveillance, but now we've got her located and we're ready to move on this worthless skunk bitch."

I was seething with anger, but I had to say yes to my boss. Backing out would look suspicious, and besides, I'd rather go after Lucy myself than let someone like McGill get the assignment to kill her.

"You're right I'd love it," I said. "I want to take that one out myself."

Moore smiled and relaxed back in his chair.

"Hays, you're sure you've never seen her, except that one time with Lizbeth?"

"Of course I'm sure," I said, looking surprised at the question. "I'll never forget that one."

"Lizbeth said you were still confused from the anesthesia. If I'm going to put you out there, I want to be damned positive you're at one hundred percent."

"That was just one small glitch—right as I was waking up. There's been nothing else since then. In fact, I feel perfectly rested and ready to go."

"All right, but don't get overconfident," Moore warned. "She and her people have killed a lot of Elites, including those executives at the Baronville Toyz store." A cruel look came into his eyes. "Hays, we want to take her alive. Her interrogation will be most entertaining. This Lucy/Megwin bitch has a lot of secrets we need to know."

Chapter 84

MY OLD PARTNER and "good buddy," Owen McGill, was waiting for me on the city's south side, at the fringe of the so-called Human Slums, or Darkness. It was already night when I got there, but McGill's height and build were easy to spot. Some things never change.

"My main man!" he said, hurrying to give me a bone-crushing hug. "Welcome back, Hays. The good times are about to get rolling again."

"Going to roll right over whatever gets in our way," I said with equally false heartiness. I was remembering how McGill had spat in my eye while I lay strapped to a hospital bed. And how he had punched me in the face.

That was another score I wanted to settle, but now wasn't the time for vendettas. Now was the time to find a way for Lucy to escape from an Agency trap, whatever it might be.

What a foul night this was turning out to be. I'd driven here with my hands clenched so tightly on the wheel that I almost snapped the damn thing off. I couldn't think the situation through because I didn't know enough about this mission, the plan of attack, or even where Lucy was supposed to be hiding. Jax Moore had told me that McGill would fill me in, then he hurried me out of his office — probably because he still had doubts about me. Moore is nothing if not clever, devious, paranoid, *and a chilling murderer.*

"You're probably thinking the skunkess is in there." McGill jerked his head toward the slum's squalid streets, which were crowded with hapless humans, plus violent Ghools — wyre addicts — moving through the smoky glow of the cooking fires. "So did we at first. It took us a while to locate the clever bitch. But we've got her, Hays. We have her nailed."

He pointed in the opposite direction, out to where the slum ended at a dried-up river channel and a dark wasteland stretched into the distance. The only structure I knew of there was the city's old water-filtration plant—a concrete hulk about the size of a sports stadium.

"That old plant?" I said. "How has she managed to sneak in there?"

"That's where we've got a small problem," McGill said. "Take a look at this."

He handed me a perspective imager, a slender mask that fit across my eyes and relayed a sharp picture of the building's interior.

I knew that Lucy would be there—but actually seeing her was like taking a hard punch in the stomach. She and two men were working at tables spread with a cache of rifles and pistols, the kind that shot metal bullets. It looked like they were cleaning the outmoded weapons, getting ready to use them.

And McGill's "problem" was easy to see on the imager—Lucy had an escape route. The plant's water mains had been opened and their maintenance hatches torn off. The mains dropped underground and branched into a complex network that ran under the entire city. At the whisper of alarm, Lucy and her team could easily disappear into the tunnels. That was certainly reassuring to me.

"We need her alive," McGill emphasized, laying a comradely hand on my shoulder. "She knows what the humans are up to. We need to know everything she knows. Actually, this should be fun. For both of us."

I studied the imager for a few seconds longer. The plant's entrances were sealed, but there was a row of grimy industrial windows about twenty feet above the ground. That's where I planned to go. I was starting to see a chance of how I might succeed — by failing.

I took one last close-up look at Lucy's face, then I set off, ostensibly to capture or kill her.

Chapter 85

MINUTES LATER, I was crouched down at the border of the dark wasteland. I had a stun-gun carbine in my hand and was tensing my legs for a sprint to the filtration plant where the Agency had isolated Lucy—I was the point man in her capture. I sucked in one more deep, measured breath. Then I jumped forward, racing in long, springing strides.

I lunged straight up as I reached the building's granite walls, catching the ledge below a window with my free hand, throwing the carbine to my shoulder with the other.

This was it, life or death. For me, and for Lucy.

I rammed the rifle barrel through the window

and aimed. Right now, this instant, I had to be the best marksman I could imagine.

Very slowly, I squeezed the trigger.

Shot of my life.

And Lucy's too.

Lucy and her men spun around toward the shattering glass. I had fired the most deliberate and careful shot—three inches off her left shoulder.

The stun blast cracked with a flash like a lightning bolt, and Lucy went reeling. But she stayed on her feet. I figured that she would.

So far, so good.

But then they didn't run for the tunnels. The three of them stumbled away in the wrong direction—farther into the plant. What was she doing? This made no sense.

Maybe I'd cut the shot too close, jolted her completely out of her senses?

I swung myself boots-first through the window and dropped in a driving rain of glass to the floor below. I needed to save Lucy, somehow—with McGill watching my every move.

Chapter 86

SHE WAS SEALING her own doom though, fleeing even deeper into the plant instead of using the escape route. And she was moving faster now too, disappearing in the dark maze of machinery, pipes, and catwalks, then reappearing for a glimpse, then disappearing again. But why go back into the building?

If I tried to chase her, I'd never catch her in time. McGill and the others would get to her for sure.

So I threw the rifle onto my shoulder again. Another near-impossible shot was needed. Could I do it twice in a row? I had to.

Very slowly — now squeeze, Hays.

The flashing stun jolt slammed Lucy to the floor. She was definitely down, but was she out, unconscious? Or had I just killed her?

I lunged forward to scoop her up and race back toward the tunnels and the way out. The Elite air-assault units were directly overhead now — I only had a minute or two left before they arrived.

Whoom! A megaforce laser blast hit the plant's roof, vaporizing at least a forty-foot section. That showed it wasn't a good idea to wage war against the Elites.

The pulsing lights of Agency aircraft appeared directly above the hole, then black-uniformed commandos came leaping through it and into the building.

I had messed up and it was going to cost Lucy. Now there was only a single option to keep Moore and McGill from getting their hands on her.

I dropped to my knees beside Lucy. Her face was turned toward me, her cheek resting on the cold concrete. Her eyes were barely open, but I could tell she could see me. "Lucy."

I drew my laser pistol and took a very deep breath. *I had to kill her!*

"Stop." Her mouth hardly moved and her voice was as faint as a sigh. But there was no mistaking the tone of command in her next few words. "Ruthless. Remember, Hays?"

I needed her to understand something. "They're going to kill you by inches! It's called a slow death. It's excruciating."

Damned if her lips didn't curl into the faintest trace of a smile. A smile? Now?

"That's what they want you to think," she whispered. "When I give you a cue — *take it.*"

There was no time for more words between us, not even a good-bye. The Elite commandos were all over the catwalk above us, starting to rappel down.

I still could have killed Lucy, and then myself, but I didn't do it.

I was clinging to her words. *When I give you a cue — take it!*

Whatever that was supposed to mean.

Chapter 87

MCGILL DIDN'T WASTE any time getting right in my face. My old buddy and partner was a distant memory, and an illusory one at that. This two-faced bastard was no friend of mine.

"That first shot was sloppy, Hays," he said. "Not like you. Are you losing it?"

"Hanging by one hand, with a second to aim and shoot?" I snapped back. "Next time, you take the shot, good buddy. I'll be the critic on the sidelines!"

Suddenly, his mask of camaraderie flashed. "Hey, take it easy," he said. "I'm just saying—

maybe you're not as steady as you thought you were."

I nodded. "You're probably right, partner." Then I turned away quickly, before he could see my sneer. No, make that my hatred of him.

I began to walk to my car, gripped by the fact that I was abandoning Lucy to slow death. The torture was a perversion of regeneration therapy. The victim's body was permeated by an electromagnetic field that sent impulses to specific areas, thousands of them per minute. But instead of healing, the impulses attacked nerve clusters with violent shocks. It was like having a white-hot probe moving inside the body, with the victim never knowing where it would stab and wound next—only that it would.

The agony could go on for weeks, and with someone as strong and determined as Lucy, it probably would. What made it even worse— Lizbeth had managed the team that perfected the torture machine. My sweet little Jinx.

Chapter 88

McGILL WAS FIRST up with Lucy in the interrogation room, which worried me. Usually I was first. What was going on? What did it mean for Lucy?

"I'm sure you aren't very bright, but you must understand that you're going to talk anyway. Why not spare yourself the hours of unnecessary torture?" he asked her, for starters.

Lucy glanced at McGill like she was looking at a slug eating garbage. She still hadn't said one word to him. In fact, she barely looked at him.

Which was amazing considering that she'd been *hanging* in the interrogation room for half an hour now, with the vicious slow death probe searing her flesh. So far, she hadn't made a sound. No moans or screams, and no answer to any of McGill's questions.

I had never seen anyone, male or female, handle the torture like this. Usually, the subject was screaming within seconds, often begging for death.

McGill looked over at Moore, who was standing behind Lucy, where she couldn't see him. Moore eventually raised a thumb, signaling McGill to up the dosage.

"OK," McGill said to her with a shrug. "You leave me no choice."

He stalked to the control panel and adjusted a setting. The next shock racked Lucy's body and contorted her face, yanking her lips back from her teeth.

Moore stepped in front of her then—and he gently touched her cheek.

"You're the toughest subject I've ever seen, Lucy," he said soothingly. "I admire that, I do. But you will end up telling us everything, and you know it. Just be reasonable. I'll make it easy on you. If you talk, we will kill you instantly."

Finally, she broke her silence, forcing out the next few words in a hoarse whisper. "I'll talk… to you…*but alone*. Get those other pigs…out of here." Her glare turned to McGill and then to me. "I'll talk to Jax Moore. Not to either of you morons."

My scalp prickled. *Was this the cue?* It had to be. But what did it mean? What did Lucy want me to do now? Stay? Fight? Go away?

I had no idea.

I was back on the edge of doubt again, and it was pure hell. Did she want *me* to kill her now?

"Of course," Moore said. "I absolutely understand why you would feel that way." He motioned us toward the door. "Both of you — go."

"Get out of here, pigs!" Lucy screamed.

As McGill and I walked out, I scanned her face, desperate for any sign that I was reading her right. Maybe I only imagined it — but I thought I saw the trace of a smile.

Chapter 89

McGILL WAS WAITING for me at the end of the hallway. His round pie face held a satisfied smile. "He'll close on her—Moore's the master at it. He'll be lighting up one of his victory cigars any minute. That human bitch doesn't stand a chance."

"No, I'm sure she doesn't," I said. I was almost shaking with tension. More and more I was feeling that I couldn't leave Lucy in there with Jax. He had all the tools of torture ever devised, and—

My head whipped as a shrill screeching noise came from the interrogation room. It didn't sound human.

Or Elite.

"What the hell was that?" McGill turned to me.

"I have *no* idea."

Then I saw a flash of light—Moore's victory cigar?

And then we both heard a terrible explosion.

By the time McGill and I got back to the room, the walls and door—all made of superstrong alloy—were shimmering with heat and spewing smoke. A thermal bomb had exploded inside— had to be. But how had it gotten in there? Certainly Lucy had been searched. Had Moore's cigar set it off?

Security guards were racing down the hall, a half dozen of them, blasters at the ready. Within seconds, they had blown open the door. Smoke and steam escaped in a searing hot fog that drove all of us back down the hallway.

"Jax Moore is dead," McGill proclaimed. "They both are. Blown to cinders."

When the smoke cleared, I stared at the disaster inside. My heart sank. The heat had been so intense that the floor, walls, and ceiling had melted half away. Everything inside had been incinerated to blackish dust and spatters of liquefied metal. *Everything.*

Including Jax Moore.

Worst of all was the empty space where Lucy had been hanging. Not a trace of her was left. She must have had the bomb inside her body— sacrificed herself. That had been her plan from the start, hadn't it?

To kill Jax Moore right here at Agency Headquarters; to send a warning to all Elites.

And I had been Lucy's unwitting accomplice. I'd done this, hadn't I?

I had captured and brought her here to die.

Chapter 90

PRESIDENT HUGHES JACKLIN glared at us with obvious High Elite rage via hologram from his penthouse—which, right now, was floating somewhere above New Lake City. The luxurious six-room penthouse was actually an aircraft that took off from the roof of the presidential mansion on ceremonial occasions. It cruised the skies as a dazzling and, frankly, obnoxious reminder of Elite power and arrogance and control.

"Moore was killed by a human terrorist?" Jacklin said angrily. "Right there inside Agency Headquarters?" Standing behind the president was—as usual—the huge bodyguard Devlin, who looked nearly as pissed as his boss.

"I'm afraid so, sir," McGill said, hunching

his burly shoulders like a schoolboy getting a scolding from the headmaster. What a toad he was; what a dangerous toad though.

I waited tensely, expecting Jacklin to demand a full account—from me—and raise the legitimate question of why Lucy had let me escape. It certainly wasn't lost on Lizbeth and McGill. I had already been interrogated on the matter—twice.

But right now the president seemed more annoyed at being interrupted than upset by the news of the Agency head's death. He had a much more important subject on his mind—7-4 Day.

"It was Moore's job to keep those despicable bastards down," he growled. "If he wasn't dead, I'd fire him. This attack shows unthinkable weakness and vulnerability, at the worst possible time."

He glanced over his shoulder into a large reception room, where a 7-4 Day meeting was in progress. His chief advisers were present. I recognized guests who were among the world's most influential Elites, dignitaries and military leaders I had rubbed elbows with in the past.

Whatever was going on at the high-level

meeting, President Jacklin obviously wanted to get back to it. The other leaders were busily placing differently colored markers on a large table that held a map of the world.

"All right, keep the Agency bombing quiet for now," he said. "These next few days are going to be insane enough without that kind of news leaking out. We'll sort out the details later. You haven't heard the last about this from me."

"Sir, I'm afraid the Agency of Change is going to need an acting chief," Lizbeth interjected smoothly. "If I might make a recommendation— I don't believe you could do better than Senior Agent McGill. He wasn't responsible for the bombing, but he's held everything together since then."

McGill? I almost choked! He was definitely mean enough, but he had nowhere near the level of sophistication to supervise the organization. Even though I would have been a stronger choice, Lizbeth acted like I wasn't even there. So what did that tell me about my wife?

The president nodded impatiently—he had other things on his mind. *Like the imminent extermination of every human on the earth.*

"Recommendation accepted," he said. "On a temporary basis. Just make damned sure you do a better job than your predecessor. Now do your job!"

"Yes, sir!" McGill said, saluting. The gesture in itself made me gag.

The hologram faded with the president striding away to rejoin his scary conspirators. By now, I'd realized what the subject must be. The top Elites were dividing up the human world, country by country. Those bastards were getting ready to take over the vast sections of the earth that would soon be deserted.

Lizbeth turned to me. Was that a tear I saw in her eye? God, she was good! "You do understand why I couldn't recommend *you*, don't you, Hays?" she said. "You're my husband. It wouldn't have been right."

"Besides, you're too valuable in the field," McGill added. "You know that, Hays. And you've been injured recently. You understand?"

I understood, all right, but I had to keep pushing on with the charade.

"Don't worry, the Agency job's the last thing in the world I'd want," I said. Then I started toward the door. "I'm going home to get some rest. I need to recharge. The big day is almost here. I'm sure it will be worth the wait."

I could feel the two of them hesitate—they wanted to keep tabs on me. But they were also wrapped up in their newfound power, and what it would mean for them once the humans were eliminated. Every high-ranking Elite would become more powerful, and probably wealthy beyond imagining.

"You've earned it, darling," Lizbeth finally said. "Wait home for me, OK? I won't be long."

Once outside the Agency building, I jumped in my car and sped straight across the city—to the human slums.

Go home, like hell.

Chapter 91

AN HOUR LATER, no more than that, McGill strode in a quiet rage along a dark, littered alley that led into a crosshatching of even more dark, littered alleyways. He was headed toward a gutted old warehouse at the far end. It was home to a collection of humans, the kind of scum who'd never had much luck to begin with. *Well, now their luck was all gone.*

"Don't come any closer—this is a warning!" a sentry, a boy, called from the shadows. The human guard was apparently used to dealing with the slum's sneaky thieves and manic Ghools—not a huge policeman suddenly charging at him like 270 pounds of battering ram.

McGill stopped short of a collision—and then

shot the human dead. He picked up the worthless boy and hurled him tumbling into the gloomy mist beyond the warehouse.

"This is the Agency of Change!" McGill roared. "Get out here now! Line yourselves up against the wall! This is the Agency of Change. You will obey me or die! I'm Owen McGill. Heard of me, skunks?"

As the frightened residents began to appear, McGill fingered the trigger of his laser pistol. God, how he hated these humans. An hour ago, he'd been on top of the world—the temporary chief of the Agency, with Lizbeth almost in his arms. Then it all blew up—because of that sonofabitch Hays Baker! That bloody traitor! That *human!*

McGill had watched Hays leave headquarters, just in case he did anything criminal or suspicious. And he sure as hell did.

Instead of going home like he'd said he would, he sped off toward these very slums. He'd lied, and no doubt that meant he'd been lying all along. He had made a fool of McGill, even as he stood by silently, allowing McGill to take Jax Moore's job as head of the Agency.

There was only one way to solve the problem,

and this was it, a job only he could do: find Hays Baker, and kill him.

"You stupid people sheltered an escaped convict—that's punishable by death, and I'm the delivery man," McGill snapped at the cowering humans. "But I'm going to give you one last chance at survival. I happen to know he's around here now. His name is Hays Baker. Heard of him? Well, where the hell is he? Anybody?"

McGill turned his most baleful glare on a young woman in rags, holding a baby tight to her breast. She seemed the weakest and most vulnerable of this pitiful lot.

"Come on, honey. Who's more important— your wee child there, or some stranger who's actually a spy?"

A gray-haired woman—the oldest, and one who didn't seem the least bit afraid of him— stepped forward to face McGill.

"She's not covering for anybody—none of us are," the old bag said. "We didn't know who he was when he was here—and we haven't seen him since. I swear before God."

McGill raised his pistol and leveled it at the old shrew's beady eyes.

"Wrong answer, skunk," he said.

"How's this for the right answer?" a different voice said—someone behind him. "*You're* the only skunk here."

Chapter 92

AS McGILL STARTED to spin around, a sharp sound—*brak*—rang out. Something smacked hard against his pistol, knocking it flying and making his hand sting furiously.

He stared at the woman now standing there with a gun in her hands.

A woman who was supposed to be dead. Hell, he had seen her burned to a crisp back at the Agency.

Except that she'd just shot the laser pistol out of his hand with one of the obsolete, bullet-shooting weapons that he'd sneered at an hour ago.

"You were blown to bits—incinerated with Jax Moore!" he yelled at her.

"Obviously not, you moron!" she yelled right

back. "I'm right here—waiting for you. And obviously, these rusty old guns work pretty well," Lucy said coolly. "If you know how to shoot. If you've practiced every day since you were seven. If you really hate your target and turn all that venom into focus."

"So you weren't blown up?"

"I think we covered that part already."

McGill couldn't believe what he was seeing, but he *really* couldn't believe what happened next. The blond girl tossed her pistol aside.

"But let's keep this fair," she said, as if that explained it.

His shock and rage exploded in a wild laugh. "*Fair?* Is that what you think is going to happen now? Hell, I'm going to rip your head apart and watch the very small brain fall out!"

The blonde frowned thoughtfully and didn't seem afraid of him. "OK, that's a bet—my brain against yours."

"Smart-ass bitch!" he yelled, lunging toward her. His massive fist lashed out in a punch aimed to pulverize her face into bloody shreds and bone splinters.

But Lucy danced aside with professional

boxing speed and agility. Then she rammed her own black-gloved fist into the pit of his belly. The strike was so hard he felt his gut crunch against his spine. Was that possible? Could she have hit him that hard?

McGill immediately doubled over, eyes bulging, and sucked for air like a beached fish on the riverbanks. He'd never been hit like that! What the hell was going on? She was a *woman,* not even half his size! Plus, he'd seen her blown to nothing with his own eyes.

With great effort he wrenched his body upright and dove at her again, his huge hands outstretched to rip her apart. Again, she sidestepped him just when he was sure he had her nailed good.

As he stumbled past, he glimpsed her whirling in a reverse kick. Now what?

What was that her boot heel slammed into his ear, smashing it and spinning him face-first into a stone wall. The impact hurt something fierce, and the wound was as much to his pride as to his hearing.

Snarling like the beast that he was, McGill fought harder. But this clever trickster of a woman was always just out of reach, stunning him with shots that hit like thrown bricks, one after the other.

As his body slowly broke down, an unbelievable reality struck him: for the first time in his life, he was facing someone faster and more powerful than he was. *A woman! A human!* He couldn't believe it. She wouldn't die. *He couldn't even lay a finger on her.*

One of her whipping kicks totally collapsed his left kneecap. With a howl of pain, he went all dizzy and crashed to the pavement. He was half-blinded by his own blood, but he could see her, looming above. She even had something to say.

"I don't feel bad about this," she whispered through clenched teeth. Then she broke McGill's neck. And then, Lucy really started to hurt the bastard.

Chapter 93

I WALKED VERY quickly, then began to run through the mean streets of the human slums, making *damn sure* everyone saw me. There was no way I could find the human leaders in this vast, complex warren—I could only hope that they would find me.

And that they would accept my help before 7-4 started and all was lost.

My oversensitive hearing caught a *pop* off in the distance—a small, sharp explosion. Weird; it sounded like an old-fashioned gunshot to me.

I calculated the shot to be 1.83 miles away— and the location clicked in my memory.

It was the warehouse where the girl Shanna lived with her ragged tribe—and where I'd helped deliver her baby, her very adorable baby, who I had promised to visit again.

Well, here I was.

I broke into a full-out sprint, racing through the crowds of startled slum dwellers, who cursed me instinctively but also shoved one another to get out of my way. They had to, since I was running at forty-plus miles an hour.

The narrow, murky alley that led to the warehouse was silent and seemed deserted at first look. There was no hint of where the gunshot might have come from.

But *something* was lying on the broken pavement near the warehouse entrance, approximately fifty yards ahead. Most of the body was hidden by a building's corner—all I could see were the feet and toes, pointing up, still moving, quivering.

I dropped to a tight combat crouch and edged forward through the shadows—tensed for any noise or movement, but especially a sudden attack.

With every step I took, a little more of the suspicious body came into view—legs, waist, a face.

Face? I haven't even gotten to the shoulders yet!
Face?
How is that—

Finally, I stared in shock at what I saw. The body's head, torn from its neck, was actually sitting on top of the blood-soaked torso.

It held a most peculiar expression, like it was still trying to figure out what had gone so terribly wrong. But the real stunner came when I recognized who the big head belonged to.

Owen McGill.

Chapter 94

I TOOK OFF again, running at half speed now, looking for anybody who might have witnessed the killing of my former partner, my former friend. The murder of an Elite agent was a serious, almost unprecedented crime punishable by slow death.

When I rounded the corner of the alley onto the next street, I spotted two women. They were a few blocks ahead, trying to hurry away. But they were slow, very slow. One was old—and the other was carrying a wee baby. I knew them.

"Shanna, Corliss," I called as I raced toward them. "I need to talk to you. It's Hays Baker. Remember me?"

I thought they'd welcome me, but I couldn't have been more wrong.

Shanna turned with a glare full of fear and fury. "I thought you were a friend!" she screamed. "You brought the cops."

I was stunned. Hadn't I helped deliver her child? "What are you talking about? That's crazy. Why would you say such a thing?"

"That agent was looking for *you*," Corliss said — calmer, but nearly as hostile. "He was going to kill us all. And there'll be more of them here now!" The two of them turned and hurried into nearby buildings.

"Leave us alone!" Corliss called back. "You're nothing but trouble. You'll get us killed."

I let them go, but pieces started clicking together in my mind. Not many people could have taken McGill down like that — only a few top Elite agents. But it was unthinkable that they'd ever turn on him. Most of them liked the cocky lout — just as I once had.

So what enemy did he have who hated him that much? And who had the courage to fight him, the skill to beat him, the strength to rip him apart?

The question burned in my mind, but no answer came. I knew that even I couldn't have brought down McGill by myself.

Suddenly, I heard the low growl of a motorbike. It was coming in my direction, coming *fast*. I swung around to face whoever was roaring up behind me. This couldn't be good, had to be bad.

As the cycle streaked into sight, the rider hit the brakes and leaned into a long, controlled skid straight at me.

"Jesus, Lucy!"

She brought the bike to a sharp, precise stop, the front wheel nearly touching my boots. Her eyes were shining, her hands were stained with what I assumed was Owen McGill's blood.

"Hays, you shouldn't be here" was her greeting.

Just this once, I shut her up. I kissed Lucy until she finally kissed me back.

Chapter 95

"SO," I SAID as we finally parted lips. "You're a lover, not a fighter. And you sure have some explaining to do."

"One of two possibilities, Hays—you decide. Either a clone blew up at the Agency, or I'm a clone. Which is it? Quickly now."

I had to smile. "I just kissed the real Lucy. I'm sure of it."

"Good guess, but I'm a *fighter*, Hays. And you shouldn't be here in the slums. Not unless you want to die for the cause. Which is what I plan to do. For real this time."

"Maybe I do," I told her. "What's going on with the resistance? What have you found out about 7-4?"

"You're the one married to Dr. Mengele," Lucy snapped. "What did *you* find out?"

My ears perked up. The distant scream of police cars was stirring the night air, and reality came flooding back for both of us. The clock was on for the destruction of humankind, and we still didn't know what the Elites had planned. Neither of us did.

"I didn't find out anything useful, and I don't see how I can now—I'm on the run myself," I said. "Let's say—Lizbeth and I are *separated*. For good."

Lucy's eyes went soft, then suddenly fierce. "We have a last chance. Here's what we need you to do. Please, Hays. Don't fight me on this. You *won't* like it one bit."

In a few taut phrases, Lucy told me her plan. Her gaze never wavered. Neither did mine— although I was chilled to the core by what she was asking me to do.

"Ruthless, remember?" she said. "This is life or death—for an entire civilization."

"I know that. It's also betrayal—of the worst kind I could imagine," I said, and nodded grimly. "I'll do what you ask though."

"Good-bye, Hays," Lucy said. "I'm sorry I didn't meet you sooner." Then she kissed me again — not a clone kiss this time either. Finally, she jumped on her bike and sped away.

Chapter 96

I WATCHED UNTIL Lucy disappeared, then I sprinted in the opposite direction, hopefully to stall the oncoming cops. I'd only have seconds to do it. As soon as they reported that I was here, they'd no doubt get orders to shoot me on sight.

Just then I spotted a couple of staggering Ghools.

They were so high on wyre they either didn't notice or didn't care about the police cars swarming into sight. I charged at the pair of punks and clamped a hand around each one's neck. Then I hoisted them high enough for the approaching cops to see.

The cars skidded to a halt and the troopers came streaming my way, guns out.

"Where the hell have you been?" I yelled like I was still in charge. "What took you so long, you incompetents?"

The lead officer stammered out a few words. "We—we got here as fast as—"

I cut him off, shoving the gasping Ghools toward him.

"Arrest them *for the murder of Agent Owen McGill!* The rest of you, find their buddies. They attacked McGill like a pack of rats. Tore him apart."

I waved them toward the woods, then walked the other way—fast. I had to do what I promised Lucy.

And she was right—*I didn't like it one damn bit.* It went against everything I had believed in— as an Elite.

Chapter 97

HOME SWEET HOME again — or maybe not. *Definitely not!*

As I stepped into my old apartment, I was hit with enough memories and feelings to make me dizzy for a week.

Right off, I heard voices coming from my daughters' bedroom. April and Chloe were here. What could be more bittersweet than that?

"Why do we have to go back to Grandmère's, Mommy?" Chloe asked.

"Remember, I told you that Daddy's not feeling well?" Lizbeth said, with tense impatience in her voice. "We've got to give him the proper time to rest and become himself again. Poor Daddy. Besides, the city is dangerous right now. I told you that, girls."

Toys

"Grandmère's no fun. She's a grump and she doesn't have enough toys," April complained.

"I'll bring you toys. But right now, we have to hurry. Let's go, girls. Now! You can bring Jacob and Jessica if you insist. And don't ever call Grandmère a grump."

They were coming out of the girls' room, so I slipped inside the front closet and partially closed the door behind me. Then I climbed straight up.

There was only a foot of space between the top shelf and the ceiling, but I wedged myself into it, folding my body like a pretzel.

It was damned uncomfortable, but the very dangerous and *humanphobic* Metallico was bustling around the apartment somewhere, and I couldn't afford to have him or Lizbeth, or especially the kids, see me.

Just being here was bad enough, but hopefully I could do what I had to do without badly scaring the girls. They'd be confused, but fine. There was no way I could explain myself to them now, only hope that someday they might understand that I had done the right thing. For humans, and even for Elites.

After a few seconds, Metallico actually came

into view. He was carrying their little overnight bags, which he set down at the front door. "Let's *go*, ladies!"

Let's go, indeed. I focused my wrist chron on his head. I'd already set it on DM—Deactivation Mode. I carried this special device because robots occasionally got in our way when we were carrying out missions. Sending out a DM signal shut them down in a hurry.

I touched the control, feeling a tingle myself as an electron pulse shot into Metallico's circuitry.

The family robot made a sound like a groan, stopped dead in his tracks, then locked in place like he'd been turned to stone. He'd be back to his old self as soon as he was reset—although if I had anything to say about it, that wasn't going to happen any time soon.

I eased out of my little niche in the closet, then dropped back down to the floor without making a sound.

"*Lizbeth!* Would you come here a second?" I called out—mimicking Metallico's sassy tone.

I could gauge her annoyance by her sharp, angry footsteps—she practically stomped down the central hallway in my direction.

"Honestly, Metallico, can't you handle something this simple on your own?"

I stepped all the way out of the closet now. Lizbeth stopped in midstep, her eyes widening in shock. I stared back at the wife who had heartlessly betrayed and manipulated me, then abandoned me to die.

But this was still the most heart-wrenching thing I'd done yet. Now I was betraying her. There was no other word for this.

"You're coming with me, Lizbeth," I said. "I'll do my best to keep you alive. The girls might not have a father much longer, and I'd like to leave them a mother. But if I have to take you dead, I will. You're just as useful either way."

"You unbelievable *bastard*," she barked. "This is our home, Hays."

"We're leaving home now. Make up your mind. Dead or alive?"

It took her a few seconds to compute her chances in a brawl against me. Then she answered with a taut, hair-tossing nod. I motioned to the apartment door. Lizbeth went ahead and reached to open it. I couldn't see what else she was up to.

Suddenly a vicious *rrrhhh* erupted behind

me — a growl like from a savage beast that's ready to feed. I whirled to face Metallico, who was charging with his steel fingers ready to pierce through my body like spikes.

"Traitor!" the robot yelled. "Human turd!"

"Nice mouth," I said. "There are children here, you know."

Chapter 98

I BARELY MANAGED to twist myself sideways, just in time to avoid being severely maimed or possibly killed. Metallico's rigid and powerful hand raked across my chest, slashing through an inch of flesh and scraping my rib bones raw.

As the powerful and determined robot lunged past me, I pivoted and kicked his legs out from under him, watching as he sailed headlong into the wall and then crashed down to the floor.

But he sprang right back up and at me again, still snarling that ugly *rrrhhh*.

Deactivation Mode, hell! I thought. The only way to deactivate that berserk hunk of silicone was to bust him up into byte-sized scraps. I'd been right all along that something was seriously scrambled in his wiring.

Now it flashed through my mind that maybe it was no accident—and that Lizbeth had secretly modified him to protect herself and the girls from me.

My darling wife wasn't standing still either— she'd taken off running toward the kitchen. "Leave me alone, Hays," she called over her shoulder. "I'm warning you."

I couldn't let Lizbeth go, so I grabbed the granite-topped coffee table and slammed it into Metallico's very thick skull. Then I went after Lizbeth. Though not as physically ferocious as Metallico, she was still just as dangerous.

But the robot was on me before I could get to her, and the two of us went into mortal-combat mode again. I was hammering him with fists and elbows and knees, while slipping like a snake to dodge his gouging fingers. The wounds from where he'd already raked me were streaming blood now, slicking my skin and staining my shirt bright red.

Through the blur of his attacking parts, I could see Lizbeth literally tearing at the kitchen wall. *What in hell is she doing now?*

Good God! She was yanking loose the controlled-fusion unit that powered all the appliances in the apartment. If she touched me with the feed-out prong, I'd be fried to cinders.

"Lizbeth — you wouldn't!" I called to her.

"I certainly will. Watch me!"

Chapter 99

I CAUGHT METALLICO'S wrist in my hands, clamped down on it with a viselike grip, and leaped up in a double backflip. Strong as he was, the torque was too much for him—I tore his arm loose at the shoulder, leaving it hanging by a single cluster of wire, which I then ripped away.

"Hays!" the robot groaned. "How could you?"

The kitchen lights flickered, and the appliances *bleep*ed as their backup batteries kicked in—*Lizbeth now had a seriously deadly weapon in her hands!*

I clobbered Metallico across the head with his own arm, then hurled it like a spear at my wife—just as she was swinging the power unit around toward me.

Metallico's spiky fingers pierced and drove through her upper arm, pinning Lizbeth to the kitchen wall. Talk about domestic squabbles.

She shrieked with pain and fury, and the power unit went clattering across the floor. I scooped it up just in time to meet Metallico's next charge.

I rammed the feed-out prong right into his chest.

Sssssttt! Sssssttt! Sssssttt! The sound was like a giant bug repeatedly hitting a red-hot grill. Very satisfying.

You're deactivated now, you homicidal sonofabitch, I thought.

I shoved the shell of the pesky robot out of my way, leaving the prong embedded in his melting torso. Then I turned back to Lizbeth.

She was still struggling to free herself from the wall, and her flesh was starting to bleed. But the wounds weren't serious, and whatever qualms I'd had about fighting her were quickly gone.

In fact, I was grimly pleased—the shock and pain might make her more cooperative.

That was when I heard a familiar little voice scream, *"Stop hurting Mommy!"*

Just then, something completely unexpected and unrecognizable came hurtling through the air, smacking me in the face. It was something furry and wiggling, and it was making cheerful *arf arf* sounds.

It took me a second, but then I recognized it as the girls' robot dog, Fuzzy! Yet another demonic toy in our house.

April, with her face scrunched up by tears and panic, was swinging him by the tail and flailing him at me.

At the same instant, I felt a sharp, stabbing pain in my ankle.

Flabbergasted, I looked down to see my little sweetheart, Chloe. She was sinking her teeth into me just as hard as she could.

"Human!" My daughter screeched the dreaded H-word.

Chapter 100

"WOOF! RARF! WOOF! Rarf!"

The robotic little mutt kept snuffling happily and trying to lick my face as April proceeded to batter me with the toy. Luckily for me, it was programmed so that it *had* to be affectionate—at least Lizbeth hadn't modified that too. Meanwhile, Chloe was still chewing on my ankle.

The nightmare I'd tried to shield the girls from was officially in session. Now it was down to damage control—getting them out of this horrifying mess and keeping them safe.

But how could I do it without manhandling them and making things even worse? It didn't seem possible. So what next—*would I have to harm my own little girls?*

Then Lizbeth stunned me in a way I never would have expected. *She took my side.*

"Girls — stop!" she said sharply. "Your father's not hurting me. Metallico went crazy, and Daddy saved me."

The girls backed away, their bewildered little eyes taking in the robot's torn-off arm that pinned their mother to the wall, his sizzled remains that lay on the floor.

Suddenly, April smiled through her tears. "Daddy, you're better!" she squealed. Then both girls rushed into my arms as if everything were back to normal.

For a few seconds, it actually was. I could have wept. "I am much better, honeys," I said. "Now go to your room and wait for Grandmère. Everything is going to be fine, I promise, and you know I always keep my promises." *I try to anyway.*

Fuzzy had trotted over to Metallico, sniffing and snuffling curiously. I grabbed him before he got zapped, and scooted him off after the girls.

With my heart aching, I watched their bedroom door close behind them. "Don't think for a second I did that for you," Lizbeth snapped. "It was for them. I love my children."

"Lizbeth, I know by now that you wouldn't piss on me if I was on fire. I'm just surprised that maybe you've got a shred of decency."

"I'll come quietly. I won't fight you, Hays. No more trouble in our house."

"Thanks for saying that. But I still trust you like I'd trust a scorpion. Probably less."

"As you should." She smiled and nodded. "Just remember your promise — to the girls."

I jerked Metallico's hand loose, drawing another gasp of pain from Lizbeth. Then I knotted a towel around her upper arm. Next, I opened the refrigeration unit and swept its contents onto the floor. The unit was just about the size of an old-fashioned coffin.

"What are you *doing?*" Lizbeth, ever the neatnik, asked.

"Get in," I said. "In!"

Lizbeth's murderous glare returned, but she obeyed and crawled inside the empty fridge.

I snapped the door shut, hoisted it onto my shoulder, and headed for the rooftop garage. Once up there, I had to ram the thing through the rear window of our family wagon to fit it inside. It still stuck halfway out, looking like the fin of a marauding shark.

Lizbeth started kicking and pounding, and I could hear her muffled yells.

"Quiet down or you'll run out of air," I yelled at her. That seemed to work, at least for the moment, as Lizbeth did the math in her head.

If there was one blessing in all this, it was that I didn't have to endure the sight of her crying. I took the station wagon airborne and flew out of New Lake City—fast and low—on the most important mission of my life. Or anybody's life, for that matter.

I was the one entrusted to save an entire civilization, wasn't I?

Chapter 101

EVERYTHING WAS COALESCING now. Or perhaps coming apart at the seams—it was impossible for me to tell. Lucy had given me a rendezvous spot in the desolate, wooded outlands to the north. As I got close, I could see that the dark glen below was gloomy and silent. So much so that I became afraid I'd made a mistake in navigation.

But the coordinates checked out, so I landed the car cautiously in the thick cover of a coppice of evergreen and spruce trees.

The instant I stepped out of the vehicle, it was like someone had flipped a switch. The forest started moving. Shadowy shapes suddenly appeared from behind tree trunks, dropped down from branches, rose up out of the brush.

Humans! I realized with a start.

They came striding toward me with assault rifles in their hands—except for a few who held short bows and had quivers of arrows slung over their shoulders. One of them bared his teeth in a wide, fierce grin.

"Hays Baker!" shouted the man.

"Tazh Khan!" I roared back. "You're here to fight. So am I!"

As we clasped forearms, he sniffed the air and his face turned serious and concerned.

"Blood of you," he declared. "You hurt?"

"It's nothing. Hand-to-hand combat. I've been hurt a lot worse. By you, matter of fact."

Tazh Khan kept sniffing, then jerked his head toward Lizbeth's prison cell, aka the family refrigerator, where she remained concealed.

"Other blood there."

"She's OK. For the moment. I'm keeping her on ice, so to speak. It's my wife. Where's Lucy?"

"Come." He and some of his men took off in a loping run. By now I'd realized that they weren't the only soldiers here. The forest was filled with moving shadows—an army of tens of thousands, men and women both, stretching as far as I could see. They must have been converging for days, landing at remote locations and traveling here covertly. Suddenly, I felt like I was in one of the World Wars that the humans once fought—I, II, or III, take your pick.

My pulse quickened with both anxiety and, strangely, pride. Humankind might not have much of a chance against whatever outrage the Elites had planned, but their courage was inspiring. It really was.

I hoisted the refrigeration unit up onto my shoulder and followed Tazh. Almost immediately, Lizbeth started to cry out, but it made no difference to me. I was committed to this betrayal.

I felt like I was carrying the weight of the world—and in all probability, that's what I was doing.

Chapter 102

I WAS ESCORTED to the human army's fleet of vehicles—armored cars and a few tanks, which were camouflaged in the brush. A cluster of jeeps and trucks had been pulled together to form a command post.

What a sight when I stepped inside! The station was crowded with the human leaders of the world—faces of those whom I'd last seen dying under ruthless Elite gunfire in France, not knowing that they were clones and all part of a master plan to fight back, to survive somehow.

And survive not just here—all over North America, Europe, Asia.

The leaders went silent for a second—then they burst into excited conversations as they realized who I was and what I was bringing to them: Lizbeth.

The real Chantal Dugare came hurrying toward me, looking even more stunning and imposing than her double had. "Hezz! How nice to really meet you!"

"How nice to see you alive," I said.

"Yes, I much prefer it that way too. You *are* very handsome, Hezz."

The crowd quieted and moved aside as she led me to the front of the compound, which had been set up like an operating-room theater. I suspected that I already knew why.

Lucy was waiting there, busily arranging surgical equipment on a table. She didn't burst out with any thrilled "Oh, Hays, you *did* it" — just flashed me a quiet smile. She'd obviously never doubted that I would come, which was high praise coming from her.

"Set it over there. I mean — set *her* over there!"

She pointed at the operating table. Then Lucy started putting on a surgical gown.

"You're going to do this operation yourself?" I said, astonished. I'd assumed that she was prepping for a physician who had yet to arrive.

"Of course I'm going to do the operation. Who else would do it?"

"Where'd you learn . . . to be a doctor?"

"From your parents—where do you think?" she said impatiently. "I didn't spend all those years just fixing roofs and gutters on the cabin. I've worked with them in the lab since I was a little girl. They taught me everything they knew. I happen to be a great surgeon. Lucky for you, Lizbeth."

Lizbeth was ready to kill, but, *hoo boy*, was this going to frost her.

I set the refrigeration unit down and opened the door so she could see exactly where she was, and maybe get an idea about what was going to happen next.

"Lizbeth Baker," said Lucy with a modest bow. "Welcome to my operating table."

Chapter 103

LIZBETH CAME SPRINGING up like a viper ready to strike. But the first thing she saw was Tazh Khan—knife in hand, and with a look on his face that said he was eager for an Elite-skin belt.

Next, my darling wife's gaze darted around to the assembled leaders, who were glaring at her like a jury at the trial of a mass murderess.

"Don't even think about touching me," she snarled at Lucy.

Lucy didn't even bother to answer. She just rolled her eyes and picked up a scalpel.

"We are not here to appeal to your conscience, madame—you obviously have none," Chantal declared.

I had never seen Lizbeth frightened before, or even nonplussed, but she definitely was now. She must have thought that she was dead and facing the final judgment—from humans.

But she caught on fast that whatever this was, it involved a fully equipped operating room. She tried to cover her lapse into fear with haughtiness.

"So you didn't really blow yourself up?" she said to Lucy with acid sarcasm. "What a pity."

"But she really *did* blow Jax Moore up, Lizbeth," I said. "She killed Owen McGill too. Two for two. So far."

That set Lizbeth back again—neither of those two were riding to her rescue. She took another look at the medical equipment—and Lucy's surgical gown.

"Don't tell me you're going to play doctor now," Lizbeth snapped.

"I just need to borrow something of yours," Lucy said calmly. Meantime, she was unhooking an anesthesia mask from an overhead rack.

"Borrow? What are you talking about? What of mine could you possibly want? We're hardly the same shoe size."

"Your *brain,* sweetie. That's what I need to

examine. Relax, you won't feel too much. Oh—
maybe you will."

Lizbeth exploded in a fury, scratching and
biting like a wildcat. But several soldiers slammed
her down and held her immobile.

"Don't you dare touch me, bitch!" she panted.
Lucy ignored the command and brought the
anesthesia mask down over Lizbeth's face.

"There, there—I'll patch you back up when
I'm done. If I have time."

A few seconds later, Lizbeth went completely
limp on the operating table. For once in her life,
she actually looked, well, trusting.

Lucy hung the mask up and turned to her
instrument tray—a gleaming selection of scal-
pels, clamps, and bone saws. I already knew that
the operation required opening up Lizbeth's brain
and connecting it by probe to a hologram imager.
The probe would then scan her memory bank for
information about the Elite genocide plan.

Lizbeth had to know the plan, or at least some
important details, and this was our only way to
find out before it was too late. It would be better
if we had that bastard Hughes Jacklin on the
operating table, but Lizbeth would have to do.

I'd managed to keep myself relatively hard-hearted about all this, but now I had to leave—go back outside with the troops and not watch the actual brain surgery. The resistance soldiers were crouched on their haunches, looking like they could stay that way for days. I stood there alongside them—and waited.

I didn't feel much pity for Lizbeth, no more than I had for McGill or Moore. But she had been my wife and mother to our children. One way or another, *this was good-bye.*

Chapter 104

I HAD NO idea what to expect next—none of us did. Not in the next few minutes or the next few days, if truth be told. Maybe the human race would end; maybe the entire planet would be finished. Hard to predict.

The minutes crept by, an eternity of waiting in a dense, thickly treed forest, which felt primeval, except for the ghostly army of soldiers who rustled around with their tense preparations for war.

Then I heard an unexpected sound coming from the command post. It started as a murmur of voices, but quickly rose to excited shouts.

There seemed to be both outrage and triumph, but there were so many languages, it was hard to tell what had just happened.

There was no mistaking Lucy's voice though: "Hays, this is it! Come in! Hays! Please come and see the insides of your wife's bloody brain."

As I ran back inside, I was startled by Lizbeth's violet hair. It was streaming away from her head like it would if she were in a windstorm.

Then I realized that the top of her skull was actually separated from the rest of her head. I knew I would take that image to my grave.

"She's fine," Lucy said. "I told you — I'm a very good surgeon. Look through — *there*."

My gaze swung to the hologram imager, where everyone else was staring. On the screen was the most horrific thing I'd ever seen in my life, and that included the film of 7-4 Day I'd watched at my parents' house.

Hundreds, maybe thousands, of Jessica and Jacob dolls were wandering through a squalid human settlement. And the dolls were *exploding* — a staccato *boom boom boom*, like from an artillery barrage that wouldn't end. Each doll was a walking, talking bomb.

Every violent flash released a fireball through the streets, along with billowing clouds of what had to be poison gas. The screaming humans, some of them small children, slapped desperately at the flames that crawled on their skin until they collapsed from the toxic vapor that seared their lungs.

It must have actually happened—an experiment maybe, a test run held in some isolated town. Obviously, Lizbeth had witnessed it personally since the images came from her memory.

In true Elite fashion, it was incredibly simple, brilliantly evil. And there were other terrifying images: simulators that appeared to give their users fatal strokes; phones that killed when they came in contact with human skulls; a vibrator, which I don't even want to describe; video games that overstimulated players to the point of death.

The assembled human leaders pushed past me, rushing to communicate the frightening information back to their nations. They were still shouting in different languages, but this time, I knew what they were saying: *Destroy the toys! Stop the Elites.*

Meanwhile, the massive human army was finally on the move. I could actually see tens of thousands of soldiers readying their weapons and piling into armored transports, prepared to launch an attack against the better-equipped Elite forces in the city.

This was Armageddon—and at least I was on the side of good.

I walked up to Lucy, who was—well—Lucy to the end. "The Elites," she said, "they don't have a chance in hell."

Chapter 105

NEW LAKE CITY was burning!

I could already see that the heart of the great city, where I had lived most of my adult life, might be no more by morning. The same could be said for the human race if we failed now.

Lucy and I began to see columns of smoke and flames from miles away as we approached the city, flying high above in Lucy's car. The fires were moving around, not just spreading, but tossing and twisting with an eerie life of their own.

"It's the dolls!" Lucy said. "Those horrid little beasts are setting whole neighborhoods ablaze. Look at them!"

"And the simulators, video games, computers,

phones—Lucy, I'm not feeling real good about this," I finally admitted to her.

She rolled her eyes. "That's just your old prejudice about Elite superiority coming through. Watch closely now, Hays. This is what we call a game changer. Look down there."

Suddenly, there were explosions everywhere I could see in the city. Small, self-contained ones. The effect was like what you see in a sports stadium when tens of thousands of camera flashes go off. These flashes went off for at least ten minutes—to the point where I had to either look away or go blind.

"What the hell was that?" I asked Lucy when it was over. "What just happened?"

"You could say it was a product recall. Those dolls, and several other toys, were very dangerous, Hays. Especially for children. But not anymore. We're eliminating the problem. I just hope we did it in time."

I looked down at the city again. There were still lots of people in the streets—humans and Elites—fighting hand to hand.

"Lizbeth helped—involuntarily, of course," Lucy said. "Those clever, second-guessing Elites had a fail-safe device in case something went wrong with their toys of death. Lizbeth told us where it was, and—*poof*. No more killer dolls, killer phones, killer simulators. There's still a problem though—big problem, actually. This war is far from over."

"And the problem would be?"

"If you want to kill an Elite, *you have to kill the head*. We haven't done that, have we? That's our mission, Hays. We've managed to throw up enough electronic jamming to cut off the presidential compound for a very short window of time. We can surprise them. We can kill the head before the body wakes. Let's go—you and I."

So now I understood our destination. The presidential mansion was just starting to glow with the light of dawn, and the flying penthouse was settling in for a landing on the rooftop. President Hughes Jacklin, that goddamn war criminal, and his upper-crust cronies would be finished dividing the world up among themselves. It was like the old human days—with the corruption of banks and Wall Street shenanigans.

A huge crowd of Elites was already gathering on the grounds below, eagerly waiting for the president to step out and deliver his long-anticipated 7-4 Day speech.

"Let's go cut off the head," said Lucy.

Chapter 106

LUCY AND I landed directly behind a parking lot, which was filled to the brim with the most expensive cars on the planet. Interesting to note, almost all of the car designs were human in origin — no one had ever understood personal transportation better, or had more passion for it. Mercedes, Daimler, BMW, Cadillac, Lexus — these were still the most desired names on hood ornaments, even for rich Elites.

"You know your way around this place, right?" Lucy asked me.

"I do. I used to work security here all the time. Let's go."

A loud, commanding noise interrupted. "You're Hays Baker. I remember you. And you — you're just some human scum."

"Actually," I said, "we're both human scum. We've come to kill the president. You have a problem with that?"

Of course he did—since he was Devlin, the president's bodyguard. At least I thought the speaker was Devlin. He was surrounded by eleven nearly identical clones of himself—just as large, just as formidable, just as threatening. I'm sure it was in vain, but I prayed the clones didn't have the same deadly level of Elite fighting augmentations.

"*We* have a problem with that. Which means that the two of you have a big problem—with us."

The twelve deadly Devlins started to close in.

"Plan B," said Lucy. "Run!"

That's exactly what we did—very fast. But the bodyguards weren't exactly challenged in the foot-speed department. They sort of reminded me of old-fashioned tackle-football players—the kinds who took massive doses of steroids. Lucy and I gained a little ground, but not enough. That's when the Devlins started to fire laser rounds, as if merely crushing us with their bare hands wasn't good enough.

"We have to take these guys out if we're ever going to get to the president!" Lucy yelled to me.

"Yeah, my thought that they'd get tuckered out from chasing us isn't working so good," I yelled back. "Got any other brilliant ideas for stopping a dozen commando-programmed behemoths?"

"Not a one."

"Maybe I do," I said, inspiration flashing as another round exploded inches from my head. "Grab a car, any car. The keys'll be there. No person in his right mind would steal an Elite's vehicle, much less from the president's driveway."

"Good thing we're just a couple of crazy skunks!"

Lucy took an oversize Mercedes pickup truck while I leaped into a sporty BMW. Both top-of-the-line, of course.

"In this case," I said to her through my combat headset as we started the cars, "it's great if you get them in the head, but it's OK to kill the bodies too."

Lucy and I accelerated back toward the armed Devlins, who clearly didn't think we had the nerve or the talent to do what it looked like we were about to do.

But we did—we had the nerve, the talent, the guts, the willpower. And besides, we were humans, and as a species, humans have a special bond with high-performance machines.

Half the bodyguards dropped to a knee in the middle of the drive and leveled their weapons.

My windshield exploded and I could hear Lucy sucking in breath over the communications link.

Maybe this hadn't been the brightest idea.

Chapter 107

I DROPPED ACROSS the seat. Metal splinters and glass rained down upon me, and the air screamed as laser blasts tore tunnels through the air where my head had been.

Fortunately, one of the many perks of my artificial endowments is a fail-safe sense of direction, distance, and velocity. Basing my actions just on my memory of the crouching Devlin phalanx, I kept my foot on the accelerator and managed a tire-burning zero-to-ninety in just under four seconds, at which point I violently yanked the steering wheel sideways and broadsided the augmented bodyguards. I killed, or at least badly maimed, six of them.

Then I went into a fast spinning turn and sped

back for the rest while Lucy joined the melee from the other side with her own truck. Four more of the bodyguards were squashed between us like grapes.

But there were still two of them—smarter, or at least faster learners, than their peers. I watched in frustration as they jumped behind cars—each in a different direction—avoiding the obvious carnage.

Great minds thinking alike, Lucy and I jumped out of our ruined cars. Even if we didn't shut down this entire operation, several Elite car owners were going to be royally pissed at us.

"Left," she said and pointed to her own chest.

"Right," I yelled.

Something told me the original Devlin wasn't among the initial fatalities, and I personally hoped he was the one I was going after now. I'd never liked that huge, haughty bastard. And I was pretty sure the feeling was mutual.

My target called out to me, "I trained with Jax Moore, you pathetic skunk," definitely sounding like the real McCoy.

"Oh yeah?" I taunted, hoping to provoke him into doing something rash. "Well, let's hope you learned your vaporization-prevention techniques a little better than he did. I heard there wasn't much left of him after we were done with that so-called interrogation."

"Let's *do* this, Hays Baker."

Just then Lucy let out a victory whoop.

"I won't go down quite as easily as my clones," promised my Devlin.

"We'll see," I called, weaving my way crabwise between the cars until I finally had a clean line of sight—and then I did something I'd always wanted to do but had never had the nerve.

I took off at full speed toward the bastard protector of the War Criminal in Chief. I got up to forty easily, then fifty, and finally sixty—which was pushing my outer limit.

He spotted me and, fortunately, his ego got the better of him. Rather than trying to gun me down, he dropped his weapon and crouched to absorb my impact. Just as I'd hoped, he wanted to do this mano a mano.

With him having easily a hundred pounds on me, and a combat pedigree I'm sure I didn't even want to speculate about, it was definitely something of a gamble on my part. At the last second, I turned my shoulder and drove into him with all my might, causing a noise like that of a wrecking ball hitting a modest-sized house.

It took me a moment to get my bearings back, and when I figured out which way was up, I felt as if I were standing on a waterbed. But as I turned to finish what I'd started—or die trying—I quickly realized I'd knocked him out cold. He wasn't moving a muscle, not even any of the ones in his head.

It wasn't the first time I'd been underestimated by a genocidal maniac in recent days.

"You all right, Hays?" Lucy called to me. "Because he sure isn't."

With that, she walked up and put two bullets into the sleeping giant's skull.

"Like I said, Hays. *Kill the head!*"

Chapter 108

LUCY AND I ran onto the main lawn, where the action was taking place. And there he was—Hughes Jacklin himself, *head* of the Elite nation.

He was wearing a dark suit and couldn't have been more serious or impressive. "My fellow Elites! I welcome you here to celebrate this wondrous and important day!" His amplified voice boomed across the concourse as he addressed the expectant, bloodthirsty crowd.

Lucy and I quickly threaded our way through the outskirts of the Elite throng. Jacklin was flanked by soldiers and other top government officials, just as he had been for his inauguration. But clearly this was an even bigger day for him, and for the Elites.

"As the sun rises on this glorious morning, so dawns a new era," Hughes Jacklin orated, sweeping his hand toward the brightening eastern horizon. "The human strain, this menace that has hovered over the earth for millennia, is about to end. They will be extinct, relegated to the same fate as Neanderthals and other evolutionary missteps that came before them. This is a good thing, a very good thing."

The crowd erupted with sickening cheers. Some of them might have heard rumors, but the president's words, in this solemn and important speech, meant that the holocaust was actually happening—extinction was happening. The shouts and applause grew louder, and the historic significance of the day was lost on no one.

Jacklin stood there, basking in Elite approval and adulation. For me, he brought to mind several important historical figures—Hitler, Stalin, Mussolini, Idi Amin. Clearly, Elites weren't proving to be much better students of history than humans had ever been.

But then he paused, squinting up at a thick, dark cloud of human transports, old-fashioned warplanes approaching from the west. They had become visible as the night sky paled into daylight—and now were encroaching over the city limits. Another historic scene flashed into my mind—*the Battle of Britain*.

The crowd kept applauding louder and louder. Apparently they thought this was some kind of air show to celebrate the supreme might of the Elite empire and this special day. They couldn't imagine that humans might actually be, dare I say it, *fighting back*.

But Jacklin was rattled. He cried out, "What the hell is going on? I didn't order this!"

It was everything the resistance had—all in this one push. We had managed the element of surprise, but if Jacklin got away and reconnected with his military command…

The surpise clearly wasn't complete. Elite jets, faster and better armed, were already streaking in from nearby bases, blasting away at their human-piloted targets. But we had the numbers, and soon the Elite planes started to go down.

Next, the air blackened with thousands of parachutes as resistance troops—humans—descended to take back the city. Suddenly, Elites in the crowd started to disperse, stampeding out from the lawn. This was clearly not on the program.

"Kill the head!" Lucy leaned in close. "Focus, Hays!"

With an earsplitting *screeeeee!* a fireball flew over the president's head, twisting and slashing like a giant whirling knife. It exploded into the mansion's elegant facade, bursting the front windows into splinters and bringing down an entire wall.

"Didn't order that either, did you—you sonofabitch!" Lucy yelled at Hughes Jacklin as she continued to rush the stage. But there were still plenty of Elite soldiers surrounding him and the other VIPs up on the dais. The bodyguards gathered around their twisted leaders, herding them to safety.

"Dead or alive," Lucy screamed, "we have to do our part! We can't let him out of here!"

Chapter 109

I UNSLUNG MY rifle, perhaps for the last time, and took off running, stooping low to the ground and circling behind the stage where Jacklin had been spewing his incredible filth and hatred. I knew the layout of the presidential compound like the inside of my own apartment: the ceremonial dais looked rock solid, but it was actually a shell with an area for housing high-tech equipment underneath.

The entrance was heavily guarded by Elite commandos, but their attention was focused on the airplane wreckage plummeting from the sky. Lucy and I came in blazing.

The secret-service men unleashed a blistering return attack. I raced like a berserk paratrooper, bouncing and flipping from side to side and somehow avoiding the hail of defensive gunfire.

I quickly spotted what I was looking for—the under-stage service entrance. But the massive steel door was sliding closed! Nothing short of an armored truck full of explosives could blast through it. That, or possibly the thermal grenade I'd strapped onto my armored vest an hour ago. I hurled it into the dead center of the dwindling opening.

Lucy yelled, "And you thought baseball was a dumb sport!"

"Don't forget *boring*!" I called back.

Phooom! A blinding flash tore through the interior, turning sensitive equipment into melted debris and jamming the door.

The gap was no wider than my shoulder, but I lunged at it, wriggling through even as acrid smoke billowed across my face. Lucy was a half second behind, with only half the wriggle necessary to follow me in.

I skidded on the floor inside, spinning with my rifle raised, ready to take on more Elite guards— whatever it took to get to Jacklin and his cabinet.

But there weren't any guards.

Instead, I heard a hoarse, familiar laugh up ahead.

Tazh Khan walked forward, his face blackened with soot. "Next time you warn me you throw grenade. OK?" he cheerfully scolded.

Chapter 110

"THIS WAY!" HE pointed. "Termite soldier scum!"

The staccato *crack! crack!* of weapon fire was ringing in the air as I burst up through a trapdoor and onto the next level. I had my rifle ready, expecting the president's guards to be there.

The first thing I saw was one of the Elite militia men. He caught a bullet and his head exploded like a sledgehammered watermelon—except it was filled with silvery microchips instead of black seeds.

"Kill the head! Like I said, Hays."

Lucy had come through like the warrior she was! She had met up with her team, and they had used their old-fashioned rifles with stunning accuracy to clear a path to Hughes Jacklin and the other leaders.

And then—*there he was!* The president spun around and stared at me like I was, well, some kind of human scum.

He stabbed a forefinger in my direction. "Kill him!" he commanded his guards, who were led by a guy I could have sworn I'd just killed—*Devlin.* Could they *all* have been clones?

The outsize bodyguard made a quick study of the expression on my face.

"Hello again, Hays," he said, stepping forward and waving the president and the other VIPs back toward a door, which led off of the dais. "You didn't possibly think I'd have been hanging out in the parking lot with my clones while my president was unveiling the dawn of our new free society?"

"Funny how one doesn't usually hear termite colonies described as 'free societies,'" said Lucy, edging forward with me and Tazh Khan as Devlin leveled his guns at us and his remaining thick-necked brethren formed a defensive wedge behind him.

There was no turning back—and there was

no delaying. We couldn't let the president escape. We had to kill the head before it reconnected with the larger body of Elite muscle beyond that door.

Chapter 111

I SWUNG MY weapon around and fired as I dove to the ground. The glowing spray of the bodyguards' automatic weapons raked the room at waist level. But my shot went wide or—was it possible? *Had Devlin somehow dodged my bullet?*

I watched in slow-motion horror as the feet of the VIPs pounded through the far doorway. After all this...

"Go ahead, be heroes for your boss," I shouted at the bodyguards as Tazh Khan, Lucy, and her platoon of human commandos took up position behind me. I'd never heard a sweeter sound than the *kerchink, kerchink* of the rounds as they were racked into the old-fashioned, but nonetheless deadly, metal weapons.

"Maybe he'll give you a pay raise in hell," I continued. "Think about it. You're outnumbered ten to one! Easily. You'll all be dead in seconds."

The Elite guards looked at the dozens of dull metal barrels aimed at them and only hesitated a second before tossing their guns aside and backing away toward the door and their escaping leadership. Despite all the deadly technology and strength of the Elites, there were advantages to fighting them: loyalty didn't stand a chance against their massive drive for self-preservation.

But one of them hadn't dropped *all* of his weapons—Devlin. As I got to my feet, he flung some sort of ceramic projectile that skimmed past my head and landed with a crunchy, thunking noise in something behind me.

As a hailstorm of at least a hundred rounds turned Devlin into a pink mist, I turned to see what the projectile was, and instantly wished I hadn't.

The weapon, a small knife, was buried to its wicked hilt in Tazh Khan's forehead.

Chapter 112

LUCY EMBRACED HER fallen friend. I'd never seen a human expression of pain that held a candle to this one. Not even my own when my parents had died.

My heart screamed at me to comfort her, but now was not the time. I leaped through the door after the disappearing Elites and sprinted into the parking area, where they were spreading out toward their vehicles.

I immediately spotted my mark, President Jacklin, running a good dozen yards ahead of the others. My God, he was running fast. Top-of-the-line-Elite fast.

He must have been doing forty miles an hour—and was just a split second from his stretch limo when I dropped to a knee and took the surest shot I could manage, right at his center of gravity.

The burst of fire hit him in the small of his back and knocked him sprawling, but I hadn't delivered anything near a fatal blow. He must have been wearing body armor. I was actually glad for it—I wanted him alive.

I cast aside my assault rifle and quickly closed the gap. He wheeled to meet my tackle in a neat blocker's stance.

And oh, how he met me. It was like running into a pile of steel rebar...that *really* didn't like me.

We grappled and rolled in the immaculate genetically modified grass of the presidential mansion.

I quickly discovered that Jacklin was enhanced more than any Elite I'd ever encountered. With some sort of double-jointed throw that sent me sprawling, he freed himself and backed up against the presidential transport, feeling for the door.

"So, my knuckle-dragging friend," he said. "You see, you aren't the only one allowed to have secret implants. In fact, I'll let you in on a little piece of classified information: I'm the most enhanced being ever to walk the face of the earth—the docs tell me I'm eighty-seven percent tech, by body mass."

"Judging by your general psychology, I'm guessing one of the first organs they 'upgraded' was your dick," I quipped. I was hoping to get under his skin and cause a distraction. But his reply rendered me the more distracted party.

"Your Jinxie could straighten you out on that matter of speculation," he said. "Personal experience and whatnot."

I tried to will my mind silent, but it was no use. How had he known her nickname? Sure, he could have gotten that fact somewhere other than from her, personally. Who knows what kind of information our fellow agents may have kept on us. But was there anything to his innuendo? I didn't want to care; I shouldn't care—there was *no time* to care!

But even as I tried to compose myself, he yelled out, "Evac!"

His security-enhanced limo immediately recognized its master's voice and sprang to life, hovering up off the ground as its doors flew open.

Oh no.

He leaped into its dark interior, and the vehicle lurched skyward. I barely managed to hurl myself after him in time to have the automated doors slam down *on my hands.*

Chapter 113

THANK GOD FOR safety features: the car was programmed not to injure any high-tech Elite hands, and the door politely refrained from severing my fingers.

"Foreign object occluding rear starboard hatchway. Please clear immediately," chirped the autopilot.

Expecting one or both of Jacklin's immaculate Italian leather shoe soles to come down on my hands, I did the most energetic pull-up of my life, heaved the door wide, and sprang into the passenger compartment.

Fortunately, the vehicle was so large that Jacklin — assuming I had missed the departure — had moved forward in the cabin to a control console of some kind. He managed to wheel around just as I tried to tackle him again, demonstrating that patented human inability to learn lessons.

"You're doomed," he said, easily dodging me. I slammed into a credenza covered in crystal goblets and decanters, all of which probably had been pirated from some human antiquities museum.

I struggled to stand as the vehicle lurched into a steep climb.

Meantime, Jacklin began to yell. "Require immediate airborne tactical assistance, alpha priority—and all forces reclaim presidential mansion im—"

Something banged into the roof of the limo and sent us both to our knees.

"You hear that!" he screamed. "You thought somehow my defense department might not manage to notice your little insurgence on the fucking presidential grounds? That's a commando squad, and I'll say it again—you, Hays Baker, are doomed! You and your whole filthy cave-evolved species!"

Just then the passenger door, which had by now resealed itself, peeled back—*the wrong way!* The noise of the twisting metal was quickly lost in the roaring wind and the noise of the jet engines outside.

A wicked-looking segmented grappling hook plunged into the cabin and dug its sharpened fingers into a leather seat. And then, as I vainly looked around for something beyond antique glassware to use as a weapon, the first commando burst through the open hatch, two pistols leveled, and began blasting away—

At Jacklin!

Chapter 114

BACK ON THE ground, Lucy and I stared down at the wounded Elite president, whose fear and disbelief were waging an epic battle on his artificially perfect face while synthetic blood and lymph oozed from the torn biotech conduits of his flesh.

Lucy covered him with a pistol as the soldiers—human soldiers—loaded him onto a gurney and strapped him down.

"We demand unconditional surrender!" Lucy snapped as soon as he was secure. "Right now, right here!"

"*We?*" he answered, regaining some composure. "You mean you represent this stinking pack of forest animals?"

I might have admired something in his defiance, except that it wasn't born of courage. Just sheer egotism and ignorance. He believed the world had somehow selected him and his kind, that somehow—despite the ludicrousness of the very idea—Elites were a *natural* evolutionary progression.

Clearly, he felt no remorse for Elite crimes against humanity, no compassion for the suffering he had caused, no accountability for the horrors he'd unleashed against us and the world in general.

"Yes, these skunks are exactly who I mean," Lucy said.

"You're doomed!" he screamed. "You already nearly destroyed the world and, without us, you'll do it all over again!"

"Shut up!" I screamed as I clamped my hand onto his throat, making sure he obeyed my command.

I leaned my apoplectic face over his and continued.

"Now listen—and I'm talking here to that thirteen percent of you that *is* still biological, Jacklin—because what's going to happen to you in the next weeks is going to make you wish you'd been born a tick on a skunk's ass rather than whatever in hell you think you are."

And then I told him what we were going to do.

It was probably needlessly cruel. And needlessly human. But hey, when I was finished, Jacklin had gone completely white with terror.

Which, I confess, made me feel pretty good.

And then I got a hug from Lucy.

And that made me feel even better.

Chapter 115

SLOW DEATH EQUALS slow torture.

That was what former President Hughes Jacklin must have been thinking one morning, three months later. He lay in an operating theater inside the vast and ultramodern New Lake City Hospital, waiting to be punished for his role in crimes against humanity. And he certainly had a very good idea what to expect next.

There was no arrogance on his face now. After all, *he* was the one in a prison jumpsuit and shackles. *He* was the one staring at the stainless steel slow death machine that was set up at center stage in the operating room.

Lucy and an impressive assemblage of human leaders, his judges and jury, stood facing him, ready to watch his sentence be carried out.

In fact, over two billion humans would be watching from all around the world.

Me? I was right there too. I was the appointed executioner of the president's sentence. And I didn't mind that duty at all. Justice is a wonderful thing—a human idea, one of our very best.

"All right, it's time," President-elect Chantal Dugare said to Lucy, embracing her and kissing her cheeks. "The world is watching to be certain that justice is delivered here today."

The world really was watching. The war was all but over, and though there would be strong pockets of Elite resistance for some time to come, they currently had no central leadership to organize them, their seemingly invincible military was severely crippled, and they were outnumbered.

The Elites began to crumble fast without having humans to serve them. They were fine overseers as long as we were doing all the labor, but when it came to things like simple maintenance, even feeding themselves, they turned out to be surprisingly helpless.

Lucy stepped forward to address the former president a final time. She was wearing a simple black dress, and it struck me that I'd never seen her in a dress before. She looked very elegant, but somber and also restrained—especially for Lucy. It was as if she was attending a funeral, a state funeral, which I suppose she was.

"You stand convicted of plotting the most heinous crime in recorded history, the managed extinction of the human race," she declared, her voice ringing out strong and clear. "Have you anything to say in your defense? I cannot imagine that you do, but this is the time, war criminal."

Hughes Jacklin tried to put on an air of authority and Eliteness, but it was difficult to do so in manacles and with the certainty of slow death coming down on him like a falling ax.

"Humans would have destroyed the planet," he finally said in a hoarse whisper. "Elites saved it. I cannot be ashamed of that. We saved *you*— from yourselves! If Elites are guilty, that is our only crime."

Lucy wouldn't let him get away with that.

"But that was long ago. And then, instead of helping us become better citizens, you enslaved and degraded us. Elites also ignored the tremendous work we've done building civilization—

including the creation of Elites. Without us, you wouldn't even exist."

"We were trying to prevent another irreversible disaster," Jacklin said, his voice rising in desperation.

"So are we," Lucy retorted. "And we're going to do it in exactly the same way—by ridding the world of your kind. Not extinction though. Something even better."

She turned to me. "Let the sentence be carried out. May God have mercy."

With Hughes Jacklin's dread-filled eyes fixed on my every move, I walked to the slow death machine. He almost looked human now, and that made this a little more difficult, but not impossible. Justice had to be carried out, and here, too, we humans had learned and grown.

My hand touched the controls, and the laser probe began its work.

Chapter 116

WHEN I FINALLY stopped the terrifying machine—after only forty-five seconds—the onlookers were so quiet, it was as if no one were in the operating theater. And yet billions were watching, in every country, on every continent.

Hughes Jacklin's face was still fixed in a stare, but now his eyes were glassy and he seemed to be looking at something that only he could see.

Then he recovered slightly, like he was waking up from a light sleep. His gaze focused on Lucy, and some kind of recognition finally dawned on him.

"Good morning, ma'am," he said with almost excessive politeness. "May I assist you in any way? Anything at all?"

Lucy answered, "Tell me your name and your job description."

Hughes Jacklin started to speak, but suddenly his forehead wrinkled with confusion and alarm.

"I—I'm sorry, ma'am. I don't—I'm not really sure." Then he looked in dismay at the shackles on his ankles and wrists. "Have I done something wrong?" he asked, as a child might.

"Let's just say that you have a debt to pay to society. And you'll have the rest of your life...to serve."

Epilogue

A BEAUTIFUL TIME TO BE ALIVE

AUTUMN WAS ALWAYS a beautiful time in the city. The mornings had a delicious chill, but warmed into mellow afternoons; the trees turned a magnificent red and gold; and the sky was more often than not a crisp, clear robin's-egg blue, which filled me with optimism and goodwill toward my fellow humans.

As Lucy and I strolled along the lakefront, I thought about my parents living here once upon a time, when they were still young. They must have done this same kind of thing and felt the same way about the natural beauty along the water. The fullness of their lives seemed to lie ahead, keen with promise, because they were poised to make a great leap of faith toward each other—what we humans call *love*.

"I just had a stroke of genius," I said. "Rare, I know. But bear with me."

Lucy smiled. "You finally succeeded in integrating quantum mechanics, relativity, and calculus into a single equation? Well done, Hays. I *am* impressed."

"Not quite that lofty, but perhaps with more of a charm factor. Let's wander downtown and find ourselves a good bottle of wine and dinner."

"Brilliant concept, maestro! Just one addendum to your theory—the food has to be loaded with calories."

The city was still somewhat unsettled from the war and the political and social upheaval that had inevitably followed. But the sterile, Elite-dominated atmosphere was slowly becoming infused with new life—human life at its best. The people on the streets didn't all look picture-perfect anymore. The rich smells of cooking spilled out from restaurants, and taverns were serving real wine and beer. There was music, boisterous laughter, occasionally a bit of disorderly conduct, and even public displays of affection.

It was like watching someone who'd been completely bland start to acquire a personality— a messy one with some bad habits, but interesting and with unlimited potential.

Then Lucy and I turned a corner, and the pleasant little cloud I was drifting on crashed against a wall of reality.

"OK, Hays. Oh dear," said Lucy. "Let's turn around. We can go another way, just not this one. C'mon, Hays—look away!"

A female maintenance worker was cleaning up loose newspaper pages and other trash on the street a few yards ahead of us. Even in her khaki uniform and without makeup or adornments, she was very attractive, and her lush violet hair stood out from a block away.

It was Lizbeth.

"Can you handle this, Hays?" Lucy asked. "I don't know if I can."

I nodded that I was OK, but Lucy slipped her hand into mine anyway, as if I were a nervous or frightened child seeking aid and comfort.

In reality, there were no worries here, nothing to fear. Lizbeth wouldn't have a clue that she'd ever even seen us before. Lucy, true to her promise, had reversed Lizbeth's brain surgery. But then, like the other top Elites, Lizbeth had undergone a memory purge and been assigned to menial labor for the rest of her days.

Still, it was as eerie as a loved one's wake, encountering her in the street like this. I'd known in the back of my mind that it might happen, but I suppose I'd put off dealing with it. I had even considered having Lizbeth relocated to another city—because of Chloe and April. The girls were just getting used to her absence, and if they saw her, it could be confusing and possibly traumatic. They clearly loved Lucy and me, but I had doubts about whether they were ready for this.

As Lucy and I got closer to Lizbeth, she paused in her work to give us a polite worker's smile. She had the same bearing as the other reconditioned Elites I'd seen—efficient but placid, with no apparent concerns beyond the minimal task at hand.

"Good evening, sir, ma'am," she said in a voice that was all too recognizable and, therefore, chilling to me.

"Good evening," we murmured, walking on as if nothing had happened.

That was that.

But then we passed an angled shop window. It gave me a brief, blurry glimpse of Lizbeth's reflection.

Maybe I only imagined that she was staring after us with her gaze suddenly gone steely — and that her hand had formed a make-believe pistol, aimed directly at our backs.

And that then, she pulled the trigger.

Also by James Patterson

ALEX CROSS NOVELS

Along Came a Spider • Kiss the Girls • Jack and Jill •
Cat and Mouse • Pop Goes the Weasel • Roses are Red •
Violets are Blue • Four Blind Mice • The Big Bad Wolf •
London Bridges • Mary, Mary • Cross • Double Cross •
Cross Country • Alex Cross's Trial (*with Richard DiLallo*) •
I, Alex Cross • Cross Fire • Kill Alex Cross

THE WOMEN'S MURDER CLUB SERIES

1st to Die • 2nd Chance (*with Andrew Gross*) •
3rd Degree (*with Andrew Gross*) • 4th of July
(*with Maxine Paetro*) • The 5th Horseman (*with Maxine Paetro*)
• The 6th Target (*with Maxine Paetro*) • 7th Heaven (*with
Maxine Paetro*) • 8th Confession (*with Maxine Paetro*) •
9th Judgement (*with Maxine Paetro*) • 10th Anniversary
(*with Maxine Paetro*) • 11th Hour (*with Maxine Paetro*)

DETECTIVE MICHAEL BENNETT SERIES

Step on a Crack (*with Michael Ledwidge*) • Run for Your Life
(*with Michael Ledwidge*) • Worst Case (*with Michael Ledwidge*) •
Tick Tock (*with Michael Ledwidge*)

PRIVATE NOVELS

Private (*with Maxine Paetro*) • Private London (*with Mark
Pearson*) • Private Games (*with Mark Sullivan*) • Private: No. 1
Suspect (*with Maxine Paetro*)

NON-FICTION

Torn Apart (*with Hal and Cory Friedman*) • The Murder of King
Tut (*with Martin Dugard*)

ROMANCE

Sundays at Tiffany's (*with Gabrielle Charbonnet*) •
The Christmas Wedding (*with Richard DiLallo*)

Turn the page for a sneak preview of

Zoo

Coming in September 2012

One

Los Angeles Zoo
West Hollywood, CA

LOCATED IN GRIFFITH PARK, a four-thousand-acre stretch of land featuring two golf courses, the Gene Autry Museum and the HOLLYWOOD sign, the Los Angeles Zoo and Botanical Gardens is more of a rundown tourist attraction than a wildlife conservation facility.

City-run and city-funded by fickle city budgets, its grounds resemble a tired state fair. Garbage cans along its bleached concrete promenade brim over. It is not uncommon to catch the stench of heaped dung wafting from cages where ragged animals lie blank-eyed, fly-speckled, motionless beneath the relentless California sun.

To the northeast of the entrance gate, the lion enclosure lies behind a slime-coated concrete moat. Once—if you squinted, hard—it might have resembled a small scrap of the Serengeti, but these days, under-maintained, underfunded and understaffed, it looks only like what it is: a concrete pen filled with packed dirt, bracketed by fake grass, plywood rocks and plastic trees.

By 8:05 in the morning it is already hot in the seemingly empty enclosure. The only sound is a slight rustling as something dark and snakelike sways slowly back and forth through a tuft of the tall, fake grass. The sound and motion stop. Then, fifty feet to the south, something big streaks out from behind a plywood boulder.

Head steady, pale yellow eyes gleaming, Mosa, the Los Angeles Zoo's female lion, crosses the enclosure toward the movement in the grass with breathtaking speed. But instead of leaping into the grass, at the last fraction of a moment, she flies into a tumble. Dust rises as she barrel-rolls around on her back and then onto her deft paws.

Lying deep in the grass, Dominick, the dominant male of the zoo's two Southeast African Transvaal lions, shakes his regal reddish mane and gives Mosa a cold stare. As has been the case more and more over the last few weeks, he is tense, watchful, in no mood for playing games. He blinks once, briefly, and goes back to flicking his tail through the high blades of grass.

The much younger Mosa glances at her mate, then toward the rear fence, at the big rubber exercise ball she was recently given by one of the keepers. Finally, ignoring the ball, she slowly leans forward to nuzzle her face into Dominick's mane, giving him an apologetic, deferential social lick as she passes.

Mosa cleans the dusty pads of her huge paws as the large cats lay together under the blaring blue California sky. If there is a telling indication that morning of something being amiss, it isn't in what the lions are doing, but in what they aren't.

Like other social mammals, vocalizations play a major role in lion communication. Lions make sounds in order to mediate sexual competition, to compete in territorial disputes, and to coordinate defense against predators.

Mosa and Dominick have become less and less vocal over the past two weeks. Now, they are all but completely silent.

Both lions smell the keeper well before they hear him jingle the chain-link fence a hundred and fifty feet to their rear. As the human scent struck their nostrils, the lions react in a way they never have before. They both stand. Their tails stiffen. Their ears cock forward as their fur bristles distinctly along their backs.

Like wolves, lions are social animals that ambush hunt in coordinated groups. The behavior the lion couple is displaying now is for taking down prey. The smell of the keeper has clicked them into hunting mode.

Dominick moves out of the grass and into the clearing. Even for a male lion, he's huge, five hundred pounds, nearly nine feet long, four-and-a-half feet tall at the shoulder. The King of the Jungle sniffs at the air and, catching the human scent again, heads toward it.

Two

TERRENCE LARSON, the assistant big cat zookeeper, props open the outer chain-link door of the lion enclosure with its hook and drags the red plastic feed bucket inside. The sinewy, middle-aged city worker swats at flies as he lugs in the lions' breakfast, twenty-five pounds of beef in bloody cubes and shank bones.

A dozen steps in at the end of the chest-high wire mesh keeper fence, Larson, a former Paramount studio lighting tech, dumps the meat over the fence and retreats a few steps. The meat plops onto the dirt in a tumble of wet slaps. Beside the open outer fence, he flips the bucket over and sits on it. He knows he's supposed to stand behind the tightly locked outer fence to watch the lions feed, but it's the July 4th weekend, and all the bosses are on vacation, so what's the fuss?

Sitting in the enclosure with the lions in the morning before the zoo opened is the best part of Larson's day. Tommy Rector, the young head of the big cat department, likes the smaller, sprier, more affectionate cats, the jaguars and the lynx, but Larson, ever since a life-altering trip to a Ringling Brothers circus at the age of seven, is a dyed-in-the-wool lion man. There's a reason, he thinks, this animal is a symbol of power, danger, mystery, why all the famous strongmen—Samson, Hercules—always had to wrestle these guys. Their power, their physical grace, their otherworldly beauty, even after fifteen years of working around them, still amazes him. Just like when he was working on films, Larson often tells friends he can't believe he's actually getting paid to do his job.

He takes a pack of Parliaments from the breast pocket of his regulation khaki shirt, and as he slips one between his lips and lights it, the Motorola radio clipped to the pocket of his cargo shorts gives off a sharp distress call beep. He reaches for it, trying to guess what the problem could be, when the reedy voice of Al Ronkowski from Maintenance comes squawking through the static, bitching about how someone's parked in his spot.

Larson half laughs, half snorts, turns down the radio's volume and exhales smoke through his nose in twin gray streamers as he scans the grass at the other end of the hundred-by-two-hundred-foot enclosure. He wonders where in the hell the two lions could be. Mosa's usually already waiting for him when he opens the gate, like a house cat who comes running at the sound of an electric can opener.

When he hears the splash, Larson flings away the cigarette and stands up. Panic.

What? *No! The moat?*

There is a raised berm and a protective platform to prevent the lions from falling into the water, but it has actually happened once before. It took the staff two hours to direct a terrified, soaked Mosa back to dry land.

That's all he needs with the bosses gone and the crew at half staff. Play lifeguard to four-hundred pounds of pissed-off, sopping wet lion.

Going into a cage without backup: definitely a no-no policy-wise, but in the reality of a work day it's done all the time. Quickly, he throws open the keeper's gate and runs to the edge of the raised berm above the water.

He lets out a breath of relief when he spots one of the green Swedish exercise balls bobbing in the moat. He forgot about the stupid things. That's all it is. Mosa somehow knocked the ball over the platform. Whatever. Whew.

Turning back around from the edge of the berm, he stops. Larson stands by the edge of the moat, blinking. Directly between him and the open keeper fence gate is Dominick, the male lion: still, silent, tail swishing methodically, golden amber eyes riveted to Larson's face. His breakfast lies untouched beside him, gathering flies. He sits there, huge, silent, staring at Larson with those flat, flame-colored eyes.

Larson feels his saliva dry up as the immense cat leans forward, then back, like a boxer feinting.

Posturing, Larson reasons to himself as calmly as he can, trying to keep his body perfectly still. Of course, the old tomcat's only surprised by his presence out here in the middle of his territory. Larson knows that in the wild, this grumpy twenty-year-old would have been long dead from defending against younger challengers who would want to relieve him of the females in his pride.

Larson figures he's in a spot of bother here. He thinks about the radio, decides against it. At least not yet. He's been in the cage with Dominick before. The old man's just throwing his weight around. He'll get bored with this little game of chicken and start eating any moment. Dominick has known Larson for years. He knows his scent, knows he isn't a threat.

Besides, if worse came to worst, Larson has the moat behind him. Three steps and he'd be over the side and safe. Wet and humiliated and maybe with a broken ankle, but by the time the other keepers arrive, his skin will still be covering his bones and his guts will still be on the inside of him, where he likes to keep them.

"There, there, buddy," Larson says—in a whisper, a *shhhhh*, baby-go-to-sleep voice. "I like your Mosa just fine, but she's not my type."

Larson senses more than sees the movement at his left. He turns in time to see something burst from the grass, huge, tawny, throwing a column of dust into the air as it rockets right at him, growing bigger, picking up speed.

The keeper isn't able to take one step before Mosa springs. Her head slams into his chest like a wrecking ball. All the wind is knocked out of him as he goes airborne and then down on his back ten feet away.

Larson lies on his back, dazed. His heart is beating so fast and hard, he even has time to wonder if he's having a heart attack. The thought goes away as Mosa's low, compressed growl reverberates beside his ear.

He reaches for the radio as Mosa puts her paws on his shoulder and bites into his face. Her great upper canines puncture his eyes at the same moment the cat's lower incisors slide with ease into the underside of his jaw.

Larson is as helpless as a rag doll as Mosa shakes him back and forth by his head. He dies a moment later when his neck breaks, with a sound remarkably similar to a pencil snapping.

Three

MOSA GRUNTS and releases the dead keeper. She uses the thumb-like dewclaw of her right front paw like a toothpick to dislodge a sliver of meat from her teeth. What's left of Larson's wristwatch falls to the dirt as she licks blood from her mouth.

Dominick, having already fed, is starting to jog for the open gate. At the end of the fenced corridor, the two pass the tiny crush cage the keepers shove them into when they need medical attention. They aren't going to miss that.

They quickly cover the length of the big cat service yard. At the far end by the hoses is a low gate with the zoo's bright white concrete path on its other side. Both Mosa and Dominick clear

465

the gate in a leap easy as a breath, and soon are racing down the zoo's promenade. The two lions spring over the turnstiles and skirt the parking lot for the nearest cluster of Griffith Park's oak and walnut trees.

They trot up a scrubby brush-dotted hill and down its other side. They catch that human scent again on a hot breeze. They spot its source a moment later on one of the golf course fairways. He's a handsome young black man in a red Nike shirt and black pants. Getting nine holes in before work. He looks surprised to see lions on the golf course.

Dominick charges, knocking the man sideways out of his shoes. His death bite takes away most of the golfer's neck in a flowering burst of blood.

Dominick releases the dead man and rears back slowly as a police car glides down alongside the fairway from the north. He can smell that there are more humans inside this shrieking, shining box. He wants to stay and attack, but he knows that this box full of humans is of the same cold, difficult material as his cage.

The two lions run for the cover of the trees.

At the top of the ridge, Dominick stops for a moment, gazing down at a distant downtown LA. Los Angeles spreads out beneath him, a brown field of humanity, woozily shaking in the smoke and gathering morning heat, dissolving into fuzz at the edges.

That smell is stronger now, coming from everywhere. From the buildings and houses, from roadways, from the tiny cars snaking along the highways. The air is saturated with it. But instead of running away from it, Dominick and Mosa run toward it, their paws digging for purchase, mouths wanting blood.

AVAILABLE IN PAPERBACK FROM MAY 2012

Kill Alex Cross

James Patterson

The President's children have been kidnapped. The water supply for Washington DC has been poisoned. Alex Cross is on both cases.

Detective Alex Cross is one of the first on the scene of the biggest case he's ever been part of: the President's son and daughter have been abducted from their school. Alex does everything he can but is shunted to the fringes of the investigation. Someone powerful doesn't want Cross too close.

A deadly contagion in the DC water supply threatens to cripple the capital, and Alex sees the looming shape of the most devastating attack the United States has ever experienced. He is already working flat-out on the abduction, and this massive assault pushes Cross completely over the edge.

With each hour that passes, the chance of finding the children alive diminishes. In an emotional private meeting, the First Lady asks Alex to please save her kids. But even the highest security clearance doesn't get him any closer to the kidnapper – and Alex makes a desperate decision that goes against everything he believes in.

arrow books

Private Games

James Patterson
& Mark Sullivan

The Olympic Games are under attack. Only Private, the world's most exclusive detective agency, can save them.

July 2012: The Games have arrived in London. Preparations have gone flawlessly and the stage is set for one of the greatest ever showcases of sporting excellence. But one man has a devastating plan. Having waited years for this chance, he is now ready for vengeance.

When Sir Denton Marshall, a key member of the London Olympic organising committee, is found decapitated in his garden, Peter Knight, head of Private London, is called to the scene. Private are working with the organising committee on the security for the Games, so Denton Marshall was a valuable client. But there is a more personal link: Marshall was also the fiancé of Knight's mother.

Having only recently lost close friends and colleagues at Private London in a fatal plane crash, this is another torturous blow for Knight. But it soon becomes clear that Denton Marshall's murder is no isolated incident, and that the killer's number one target is the Games itself.

arrow books

We support

National
Literacy
Trust

I'm proud to support the National Literacy Trust, an independent charity that changes lives through literacy.

Did you know that millions of people in the UK struggle to read and write? This means children are less likely to succeed at school and less likely to develop into confident and happy teenagers. Literacy difficulties will limit their opportunities throughout adult life.

The National Literacy Trust passionately believes that everyone has a right to the reading, writing, speaking and listening skills they need to fulfil their own and, ultimately, the nation's potential.

My own son didn't use to enjoy reading, which was why I started writing children's books – reading for pleasure is an essential way to encourage children to pick up a book. The National Literacy Trust is dedicated to delivering exciting initiatives to encourage people to read and to help raise literacy levels. To find out more about the great work that they do, visit their website at www.literacytrust.org.uk.

James Patterson